ONE BROKEN LIFE

ONE BROKEN LIFE

P.I.V.O.T. LAB CHRONICLES™ BOOK SEVEN

MICHAEL ANDERLE

LMBPN Publishing
PMB 196, 2540 South Maryland Pkwy
Las Vegas, NV 89109

First US Edition, January, 2021
(Previously published as a part of the Megabook, *No Time To Quit*)
eBook ISBN: 978-1-64971-413-8
Print ISBN: 978-1-64971-414-5

THE ONE BROKEN LIFE TEAM

Thanks to the JIT Readers

Billie Leigh Kellar
Dave Hicks
Deb Mader
Diane L. Smith
Jeff Eaton
Jeff Goode
John Ashmore
Kelly O'Donnell
Kerry Mortimer

If I've missed anyone, please let me know!

Editor
The Skyhunter Editing Team

CHAPTER ONE

"You're not *happy*, though," Mike said flatly. He stirred his coffee without looking up. "I don't think so, anyway."

Ben fought the urge to sigh. For someone as terminally non-confrontational as his friend was, this was the equivalent of flipping a table. He had never once seen the man yell at anyone. If Mike was pushing back at all, he should listen.

He looked at his plate. Half of his pancakes still remained, sprinkled with the sugar he used instead of maple syrup. Eve had referred to that as a crime against breakfast. It was one of the litany of incompatibilities that had led to her walking away.

Probably not the main one, he reflected.

"What do you think would make me happy?" he asked finally. He cut off a chunk of pancake with the side of his fork and stuffed it in his mouth. "Ah why duhoo thig *ibot?*"

"I don't know what would make you happy," the other man said. "I'm not in your head. And I didn't understand the second question at all."

Ben washed the mouthful of pancake down with weak coffee and winced at the heat. This diner—like many he had come across—apparently believed that if they made the coffee hot enough, no one would notice that it barely resembled the expected flavor.

It was more like hot water someone had told about coffee, honestly.

"I asked why you think I'm *not* happy," he said after pounding his chest.

"I know you, remember." Mike cut a piece of his omelet. "I know when you're not happy. And it's been four years. You used to be so fired up about using your degree and now—"

"Now there are no jobs," he reminded him. "Remember that? The whole big economic crash? Too many people with advanced degrees?"

"There aren't enough jobs," the man conceded when he had finished chewing, "but there's one for you."

He snorted into his coffee.

"You were the valedictorian," his friend told him. "Your professors loved you, they were falling all over themselves to write letters of recommendation for you, and you're seriously telling me you haven't found a single job opportunity in four years?"

"I haven't been looking," he said.

"Exactly!"

"Look." Ben leaned forward. "I'm not gonna take a job I hate merely for the chance to find a job I *kind of* like at *some* point while living in a shitty apartment with three other people."

Mike sighed, leaned back, and rubbed his face. "I'm trying to help," he said finally. "You know that, right?"

"And I don't want help," he said.

"Ben—"

"What I *want*," he said, talking over him, "is to have a good climb before you go back to tiling bathrooms and painting walls and...I don't know, planning flowers. Whatever people do for weddings."

It was a cheap shot and he knew it. His friend was equally

happy and scared to be settling down with Natasha, and he had promised to be good about it.

"You would know what was going on," Mike said patiently, "if you ever came to game night. Or…lived closer."

"*Again*—crappy job, crappy apartment, no thanks."

"Or you could read the emails I've sent you about it. If you intend to hop all over the world, you might at least be on Facebook or something."

"Nope," Ben said unrepentantly. "First, many places don't have Internet. Second, I don't have a camera, and third? I don't care what level so-and-so got to in Call of Duty or what someone else had for lunch. I want to *live*."

"There are many ways to live, man." Mike was used to these tirades so he took them in stride. He pulled the check to him and put cash down, waving Ben away. "Nah, I've got this one."

"Don't you get all pitying with me. I'll find another job soon."

"Ski instructor?" the man suggested.

"After taking care of polar bears, nothing else with snow lives up." He pushed his way out of the booth and they moved to the door.

"Mountain tour guide?"

"Wandering slowly up mountains at the pace of a diseased sloth? I think not."

"Cowboy?"

"Now you're talking." Ben grinned as he picked his helmet up and settled it over his head. Their motorcycles were next to one another, both sets of paniers stuffed to the brim with camping and climbing gear. Today was their last stop before Mike returned to Boulder and he headed to Denver to leave his motorcycle with his parents and decide where he would go next.

The two men set off without further conversation. They both knew their destination and the coffee was still kicking in. Their route wound through the foothills and Ben streaked past a couple of eighteen-wheelers that engine-braked their descent with puffs of black smoke. The road began to rise more sharply. As he wove through patches of shadow and sunlight, the dry air switched from hot to cold and back with surprising speed, and he took the time to enjoy the wind on his skin.

Too cold, too hot, too sunny, too rainy—he had seen all of it in the past four years. He'd been hired to look after equipment and feeding stations on a polar bear preserve, helped dig a series of wells in Guatemala, and snorkeled in Greece. His life read like the bucket list no one ever accomplished. If somewhere had a crazy local food, he had probably tried it. If a mountain had a spectacular view, he had probably climbed it.

Except Everest. Who had the spare cash for that?

So Eve was gone and he didn't have another job lined up right now. He would be fine as he always was. Mike knew that.

It wasn't like this was where he'd planned to be when he started on his PhD, or even when he'd finished it. He intended to be a professor—or maybe tackle the issues around industrial farming, or, or, or... There had been so many things he was excited about.

The job market had beaten that out of him with a very heavy baton in record time. One astonishingly bad postdoc position later, Ben had fled to the polar bear preserve in northern Canada.

He was still of the opinion that the polar bears were nicer than most of his bosses.

One thing had led to another from there. Eve had gone with him, and to Guatemala, which they had both liked, but she wanted to settle down. She wanted a house with air conditioning and a job with regular hours and stable pay.

To achieve that, she was willing to give up the gorgeous sunrises and the aching muscles, and he simply wasn't. Every day, he felt a little farther away from the labs he'd planned to spend his life in. Their breakup had been ugly and he hadn't dated anyone seriously since then. Every time he looked at his friends' lives, with the job frustrations and the TV shows and the tiny apartments in gray cities, he couldn't understand it.

To him, that seemed reasonable. Mike, on the other hand, had called him a "sanctimonious bitch." More than once.

By the time they stopped at their climbing route for the morning, Ben was buzzing with the effects of the coffee—which forced him to concede that maybe there had been some legitimate caffeine in it. They donned their harnesses and examined the various routes currently marked by iron rope hooks.

"You know," Mike said a shade too casually, "Josh was saying he had a room to rent. And he'd be away a lot."

"Josh…"

"Spring?" The man gestured above his head. "Super-tall, blond hair."

"Oh, right. Why is he away a lot?"

"He's in the Air Force." He was definitely too casual now. "He was saying they have a number of job openings for people in STEM and practically drooled when I mentioned that you—"

"Nope." Ben pointed chalky hands at his friend. "The last thing I'll do to get a job is to join up with some ridiculous chest-thumping org that basically wanders around having dick-measuring contests with every other country."

Mike paused in the act of taking a sip of water. "I didn't understand any of that."

"You know what I mean."

"I don't."

"Who has more tanks, who has more aircraft carriers, or who has the best technology. It's us—it's always us—and the last thing we need to do is waste our time solving problems that don't even exist for wars that won't ever happen. And even if they did, lining people up and pitting them against each other until you run out of people is…what's the word I'm looking for? Fucking stupid."

"Interested in military jobs?" Mike mimed writing on a notepad and made an X in the air. "No."

"I'm merely saying there are better ways to solve problems."

"Uh-huh. Like maybe not having them start because you headed them off at the pass?"

"I sense you're trying to slow-walk me to an epiphany," he said grumpily. "Save it. It's climbing time."

"Right." The other man rolled his eyes. "So, who's going first?"

They climbed until around noon, at which point Ben was so hungry he thought his stomach would devour itself. He rappelled down and brushed the chalk off his hands to where Mike unpacked sandwiches.

"When did you get those?"

"I stopped at the store before leaving town," his friend said as he picked them up and examined them. "Ham that looks like turkey, or beef that looks like—you know what, let's throw that out and share the ham."

"Good call." He sat and watched the sun play over the rocks. After he'd chewed contemplatively for a few minutes, he said, "You know, you'll love that house."

Mike looked at him. "You think?"

"Yeah. Natasha showed me the sketches last time I was there. I'll help you with some of the stuff if you want. Landscaping, or whatever."

"I'd like that."

"And I'll even help with centerpieces or wedding dresses or whatever the hell it is."

"Ben—"

"It's not that I don't *want* to hang out with you guys," he said. "It's only…there's no place for me there right now."

Mike said nothing. He wrapped his arms around his knees and stared at him.

"The only time I feel alive is when I'm outside," he explained. "I forget about the loans, the commutes, car trouble, all the stupid shit that piles up… This is the only place where the world makes sense to me."

"I get that." The man smiled. "But if there's one thing I've learned, it's that there's no surefire way to make life simpler. Sometimes, you gotta wade into the muck to get to the parts you want. And I don't think you want to spend the rest of your life climbing mountains. I think there's more you want to do."

He shrugged. "Maybe. But I do know that climbing is what I want to do for the rest of the day, and I heard about another route—gimme that map, I'll show you—here. The views are supposed to be fantastic. Come on."

CHAPTER TWO

The burning in her fingers told Eliza that she'd zoned out. She swore and yanked her hand away from the cheap coffee cup, which didn't do nearly enough to protect against scalding hot coffee.

"Crap." She examined the tips of her fingers, which were an angry pink, then wrapped the edge of her fleece jacket around the cup to get it to the table. Her eyes felt scratchy, as did her throat and her scrubs.

Why had she agreed to do a double shift, again?

She knew why. It was so Leslie could go to her brother's wedding, which had seemed reasonable when the woman asked about it a few weeks earlier. Some extra hours were easily doable. Anyone could make it through a few extra hours, right? Especially at a fairly out-of-the-way ER. Aspen, CO, only had a run of injuries during the winter, when every idiot and their next-door neighbor came to ski.

Or that was how it usually was, but it had been a hellish few weeks between an outbreak of something flu-related and a higher than usual number of home renovation related injuries.

She had made a personal vow earlier today never to use a nail gun. Even the thought of it made her shudder.

Eliza opened the cabinets in the break room in search of anything vaguely food-like. A box of granola bars was the first thing she saw that was edible, and she snatched one and stuffed as much of it in her mouth as she could.

Consequently, she looked like a sleep-deprived chipmunk when Todd burst into the room.

"All hands on deck!" He gave her a look. "Okay, chew first. Then all hands on deck."

She swallowed, choked, tried to wash the granola bar down with scalding coffee, and pounded her chest. When she recovered, she leaned against the counter and winced. "What happened now?"

"Guess." His favorite games were the darker ones.

"Sharknado?"

"Close." He waited for her to gulp the rest of her coffee—burned tongue be damned because she would need it—and move into the hallway with him, where they both broke into a jog. "Climbing accident."

"Oh, fuck." Rock climbers came from all over the United States to try various Rocky Mountain routes, and their injuries tended to be about as bad as car crashes. "What are we looking at?"

"Two adult males in their early thirties. One seems about as close as you can get to undamaged after falling off a mountain and the other…looks damned bad. I'd say five or six broken bones? Maybe more? There's blood everywhere."

The other staff members were taking their places around tables as they dashed into the room and scrubbed up. She was pulling her gloves on when the team came in the door, and her heart dropped to see how injured the patients were. Even the one who seemed "undamaged," in Todd's words, was bruised and scraped extensively.

She wasn't sure how long it was before her patient was wheeled away, but she slid down the wall and onto the floor as soon as the gurney was gone, pulled her mask down, and exhaled in a whoosh. Across the room from her, slumped in an identical position against the far wall, Todd nodded. Beside him, Kyle lay on his back with his hands over his face.

Her arms, gloves, and scrubs were covered in blood. It was all a blur of tests, cleaning wounds, stitching wounds, setting bones, and holding her hands carefully to avoid jostling the man's head. Todd said the patient was in his early thirties but he looked younger. Then again, everyone did when they were passed out on an OR table. They looked delicate and vulnerable.

But he was stable. Eliza sighed and tried to find the energy to stand. She could do it. She could.

Maybe in a few minutes.

Wearily, she leaned her head back again and had begun to relax when one of the next-shift doctors poked her head into the room.

"What's this about a weird neurological episode?"

"Dunno." She yawned. "I kinda had an"—she gestured at her bloody scrubs—"episode of my own to deal with."

"Yeah, one of the climbers?"

"I don't know anything about a neurological problem," she said and frowned. "Todd, did we do an MRI or anything?"

"Not on ours," he confirmed. "We were too busy setting bones and there was no indication of a brain bleed."

Eliza was curious now. She stood without thinking about it too much, steadied herself on the wall, and followed her colleagues into the hall. A few of them were clustered around a set of scans. She and Todd stood on tiptoe to crane over their shoulders.

"Has he woken up yet?" someone asked.

"They're keeping him under until they know if the bleed is

still active." The doctor holding the scan tapped on it. "And not only there either. It's here too."

"Parietal lobe damage," Eliza murmured to Todd, who still couldn't get a clear look. "Aaaand the spinal column. So much for not being damaged."

"Something about bloody wounds gets my attention, what can I say?" He shook his head as they moved toward the coatroom. "Well, I guess we'll see. I hope he wakes up—if he doesn't, we won't find out what the problem was."

"That's gross." She elbowed him. "Have some respect."

"Hey, TBIs are the way we learn about the brain." He shrugged.

"Not with confounding variables, they're not." She stumbled. "God, I'm *exhausted.*"

"Don't you live way out in the boonies?"

Eliza groaned.

"Come sleep on my futon. Come on." Todd ushered her out the main door.

"Are you sure?"

"I live three blocks from the hospital. Why do you think I bought a futon? It's for you cretins when you can't drive. If you feel bad about it, buy me lunch."

"Do you think we'll be awake by lunchtime?" She raised an eyebrow. "You're ambitious. I plan to pass out for at least ten hours."

They pushed out into the morning cold in time to see a family almost fall out of a car. A tall, lanky woman with curly hair stood with two older couples. All of them had the exhausted, adrenaline-burst look of families who had received a call in the middle of the night. She watched the younger woman usher them all into the hospital and then struggle with the suitcases.

With a sigh—more weary than annoyed—Eliza and Todd went to help her.

"Thanks," the woman said. Her gaze traveled their dirty

scrubs. "I—thanks. I don't suppose…" She swallowed, looked quickly at the door, and focused on them again. "I don't suppose you know how the two climbers are."

They were used to this awkward kind of question—the one you weren't allowed to answer but you did anyway.

"I'm Mike's fiancée," the woman explained. She looked from one to the other with barely controlled desperation.

Eliza didn't have the first clue which one was Mike. "They're both stable," she said because that much was true.

"And—"

"We'll bring your bags in," she said before the woman could ask any questions she didn't want the answers to. "You go catch up."

She and Todd hauled the bags inside to the desk and left with a wave at the greeting clerk. They didn't talk for most of the way to his apartment, and it was only when he was unlocking the door that he said, "This shit makes me want to never get married."

Surprised, she looked at him and waited for him to continue.

"Whichever one's her fiancé, the whole thing's fucked now," he said. "There'll be no wedding this year, not with either one of them. And what about the parents?"

"I'm not sure I follow."

Todd was silent while they walked into the room, and he shrugged. "I get through it every day, but all the shit I see—I don't think I could deal with it if it were someone I loved."

"You wouldn't ever have to operate on your wife, though," Eliza pointed out.

"It's not that." He shook his head and pulled takeout containers out of the fridge. "I hope leftover Chinese is good with you. It's all I have."

"That's fine. Thanks." She opened some of the cartons and put them in the microwave. "So, what *do* you mean?"

"I guess I mean…you become a doctor and you start to see all the fucked up shit that happens to people." He shrugged again. "I can't imagine walking into a hospital and seeing someone I cared about laid out in a bed, looking like either of those two guys. It would rip my heart out."

"Oh." She folded her arms. "I hadn't thought of that."

"Simply watching the future you thought you had go up in smoke," Todd said. He stared at the opposite wall, lost in thought. "Either it's the one we treated—and God knows if he'll ever walk again—or it's the other one, and what if he *does* wake up and he's never the same?"

"Hey." Eliza looked at him with concern. "Are you okay, man?"

He took a deep breath. She'd never seen behind the veneer of jovial dark humor before, but now that she could see the cracks and the fear beneath, she didn't think she'd ever be able to unsee it.

"I got into this because I wanted to help people," he said. "Now we're in our residency, I know what I'm supposed to know and it's hitting me how much we…can't fix." He forced a smile. "I don't think I've ever felt more helpless than I do these days."

"Okay." She opened cupboards until she found water glasses and filled one. "Drink this."

"What? Why?"

"Do it." She pulled one of the containers from the microwave. "Now eat this. All of it."

He complied, his eyebrow still raised.

"Now, go," she told him and pointed in the vague direction of where she assumed his bedroom was. "Food, water, and sleep."

"That won't help."

"It won't hurt," she corrected. "Because when you wake up, they need you in that OR for the next time someone comes in like those two."

"Do they?"

"Yes." Eliza took him by the shoulders and looked him in the eyes. "Because we're not the only ones out there who can fix them, but if we don't stabilize them, if we don't get them to stop bleeding out, and if we don't get all the bones set, they'll never have a chance at all. You did your part tonight. Go to sleep."

For a moment, she thought he might cry. He pulled her into a hug and nodded. "Thanks," he said, his voice muffled. "The futon's in there."

"Cool. And do you have any spare clothes?" She gestured to her the bag with her scrubs. "Because I need to get these washing. It probably wouldn't make anyone feel good to see me come in later still covered in blood."

Natasha was sleeping, her head on the edge of Mike's hospital bed, when his parents returned to the room. She sat abruptly and looked hastily to see if a noise from her fiancé had woken her. When she pressed her fingers to her forehead, she felt the imprint of the blanket.

"Why don't you lie on the couch?" his mother asked her. Monique Parker kept her hair cut in a gamine French bob, and everything from her chic clothing to her lingering accent reminded her of the woman's Parisian upbringing. She didn't have a hair out of place, even now.

"I, uh…" She ran her fingers through her curls, which would never, on a good day, look as neat and presentable as the older woman's hair. "Sure." She swallowed. "How is Ben? Did you see him?"

Mike's parents exchanged a look.

"Oh, no," she said. "Oh, no. What's wrong?"

Monique looked at her son's sleeping form, then sat and gestured for her to do so as well. "I know how close all of you are," she said.

It was true. The two men had grown up together, and she had joined the group in college. They had all been friends for years before Natasha and Mike fell for each other, and she still sometimes felt guilty. It felt like they were leaving Ben behind.

It was part of why she'd encouraged Mike to go on this trip with his oldest friend, and if Ben was now injured beyond recovery… She didn't want to think about that.

Natasha pressed her hands over her mouth. "You can tell me," she said as steadily as she could. She looked at her fiancé and the bruises and stitches and casts. *It can't be much worse than this.*

"They think there's some brain damage," Monique said. "There's a bleed in a section of his brain. It seems to have stopped and they'll wake him tomorrow. But they don't know…" Her voice trailed off.

She curled her hands into fists so tightly that she thought her nails would break the skin on her palms. *They don't know if he's still in there,* her mind finished for her. She looked at Mike again and her lip trembled. When she had gone to bed the day before, she'd looked forward to her wedding and renovating the new house.

Now, she was close to losing the two people she cared about most in the entire world.

CHAPTER THREE

Ben wasn't aware of anything until he opened his eyes. He remembered that sunlight had turned his eyelids red for some time and for one moment, everything was perfect. The bed was soft, the room was shades of pale, and there was the distant sound of voices.

Then, the smell hit him.

It was one every hospital had—sharp at the edges and a combination of disinfectant, metal, and linoleum. Behind it lurked the smell of vomit that was no longer there but you could still somehow tell. Old blood was another distasteful addition.

So many things beeped too. He hadn't noticed it, maybe because he was so used to the sound at this point, but he heard it now and the number of different beeps was dizzying. Instinctively, he wanted to put his hands over his ears but couldn't.

He tried to roll his head. At first, it didn't move at all. Then, it flopped abruptly forward all the way. The headache came in a burst of tenderness near the back of his skull and down his spine. He yelled—not entirely voluntarily—and tried to make his head return to the position it had been in but he couldn't do that either. It took everything he had and long moments of struggle while the blood flow to his head constricted and his breathing became shallow. The beeping increased in speed until he heaved his head back with all his strength.

It thumped against the pillow and he yelled again. The pain was intense. It was only a pillow, but the touch of it against him felt like someone had hit him with a club.

Ben wasn't sure if he blacked out. What he was sure of was that he saw the fall again. Mike's body had hurtled toward him and impacted with the stone face, blood already pouring from his nose and his arm tangled in the line. He relived the realization that he was falling too and the adrenaline rush that punched him in the solar plexus as he tumbled.

He didn't remember hitting the ground, though. A memory surfaced of his eyes open again while people crowded around him. An oxygen mask was pressed over his face so he felt like he was suffocating and his breath sounded mechanical.

Everything hurt beyond belief.

The image flashed to darkness and the sound of helicopter blades.

Yes, he remembered that. People called to each other over his body exactly like this, while he couldn't move or speak in the dark and the feeling of being terribly, utterly alone swept over him. He had known he could slip away and none of them would be able to stop it.

And then—somehow, this was the scariest part and made his mechanical-sounding breath shallow—he had slipped away. He didn't remember passing out, but he had. The odd thought crept in that he might never have woken up and he wouldn't even have realized.

He didn't mean to hit anyone. In all honesty, he didn't mean to do anything and was merely so afraid. His whole body came off the hospital bed and the sound of a scream was definitely his because everything hurt so badly before he fell sideways. People in scrubs caught him and someone yelled something about the fucking side rails not being in place. His head was near the floor and lines of bright pain seared across the backs of his hands and into what felt like bars on his arms. He'd thrown his arms and legs and the limbs had flailed uselessly from their sockets without his control.

They manhandled him into the bed and he could see they were scared. They thought he was fighting them.

"—m not," Ben managed to mumble. He wasn't trying to hit them, hadn't wanted to fall out of the bed, and wasn't trying to do any of this. "I'm not." But the words came out garbled behind the mask and his body wouldn't stop moving.

A cool sensation on his hand and another bright prick of pain brought the realization that he'd dragged the IVs out when he fell. In the next second, something hot washed through his arm and he went blessedly limp.

Good. Thank God. He hadn't wanted to move like this. Nor did he want to hurt anyone—not them or himself.

He'd seen the bruises and the cuts and oh, God, what had happened? What was going on?

"Mike!" The word burst out of him with all the force in his lungs.

Which, after so many years of working outside every day, was a significant amount of force.

Once he started yelling, he couldn't seem to stop. His mind was full of words and questions. *Where is Mike? Is he okay? How did people find us? What's wrong with my arms?* But his stupid mouth wouldn't cooperate and simply shouted the same thing repeatedly. "Mike! Mike! Mike! *Mike!*"

They held him down now. He was angry about that but also ashamed.

Finally, he saw a familiar face. Natasha. *Thank God.*

"Mike!" *No, you idiot. Natasha.* "Mike!" He would have to hope she understood.

"Ben. Ben! Ben?" She leaned over the bed and put a hand on

his chest and he roared with pain. "Oh, God—I'm sorry. Ben, can you hear me? Mike is okay. He's okay, Ben. Mike is okay."

He slumped against the bed, coated with sweat now. "Mike." His voice sounded like it came from very far away. "Mike."

"He's okay, Ben." Natasha's face swam in his vision. It seemed to be moving wildly and he couldn't focus on it.

His stomach didn't feel so good.

"He's okay," he heard again.

"Mike…"

The drugs took hold and he went under.

"Jesus," Todd said with raw emotion when they were far enough away to speak without the family hearing them.

Eliza nodded, horrified into silence. All she could think was that at least his parents hadn't been there at that moment. She couldn't stop herself recalling what her friend had said about how difficult it was to see people injured like that, or frightened and in pain.

And these weren't even people they knew.

Leslie joined them in the break room a few minutes later. She had, as usual, one of her adorably-arranged lunchboxes—a hobby of her fiancée's—but she didn't look like she had any interest in eating. She sat at the table and looked shell-shocked.

They all sat for a moment in silence. The ER had returned to its usual functioning today, which would have been a relief under normal circumstances.

Right now, it meant they didn't have a distraction from what they had seen.

"So, what do you think it was?" Eliza asked finally. She looked at Todd and hoped he saw the plea in her eyes. *Please make a joke. We need to joke about this.*

Thankfully, he picked up her cues. He mimed smoking a cigar

and stroked an imaginary goatee. "Velllll," he said and drew the word out. "I vould heff to say—"

"Why are you being German?" she asked.

Leslie stifled a laugh and at last, opened her lunch box and removed two adorably patterned matching chopsticks.

"You know, I don't know." He looked at them. "He was worried about his friend and remembered his name, so that's good brain function. And there's a lot we could chalk up to pure shock at this stage."

Eliza nodded and went to get another cup of coffee. "Something weird happened with movement...but the bleed wasn't in the motor cortex."

"That's the thing." He rubbed his nose. "What the fuck does it all mean?"

Leslie held one hand up and motioned to where she was chewing. She swallowed hastily. "Proprioception," she said. "Kinesthesia—where your body is in space."

"I know what proprioception is," Todd said and sounded offended. "But how..." He scratched his head.

"You know how babies walk?" the woman asked. "They'll look down constantly and then fall, or they put their feet down hard and pick them up too high, right? They're still learning where their body is in space. It's why teenagers get so clumsy."

"Oh, so there's a scientific explanation for how I was at sixteen. That's good to know."

She grinned. "The other thing is you'll see them doing things like looking at their hand while they wiggle their fingers. They're learning how to control their muscles and looking at them helps."

"Really?" He nodded. "I always thought they were simply tripping balls."

Leslie laughed. "Maybe it's that. Anyway, learning how to control muscles *without* seeing them is a big skill."

"Okay, but he did learn," Todd said. "Or...whoa—wait, are you saying it's all been wiped?"

"I don't know." The woman made a slow-down gesture with her hands. "But that would be the parietal lobe, and it does happen. There are adults who lose all proprioception and sometimes, it's not even trauma-related."

"Great," he said to Eliza. "More things to have nightmares about."

She grinned at him. As much as he decried her water-food-sleep plan, it almost always worked to put people in a better frame of mind. It was her version of IT telling someone to reboot their computer.

It was good to see him back to his old self.

"What's the treatment?" she asked. "If that's the problem."

"Uh…" The woman grimaced. "There isn't one? Okay, there are kinesthesia drills that some athletes do and those work fine, it's only— Well, I'm not saying it doesn't get *better*. It's merely learning all your proprioception all over again."

"And an adult's brain isn't wired for that," Todd murmured.

"That, too," Leslie agreed.

"Frankly," Eliza said, "having met a few babies, I have to say I'm not sure *their* mind is wired for it either. Have you met any? They cry. A *lot*."

The other woman grinned as she took a bite. "I'll have you know that Kate and I are talking about trying."

"No." She almost dropped her coffee. "For serious?"

"For serious. She says she's willing to go first." Leslie gave a smile that was half-happy, half-terrified. "I spent the plane ride back looking at sperm donor…report things."

"Any rocket scientists?" Todd asked. "Ooh, what about, like—super-spies?"

"Yeah, I'm sure many super-spies donate sperm in Aspen," she retorted. She raised an eyebrow. "It must simply be bad luck that we haven't come across one yet."

"Damn." He grinned. "You can't win 'em all, I guess. Okay, kiddos, back to the grind."

"I'll come with you," Leslie said. "Eliza, you take the next lunch."

"Thanks." She went to the fridge and retrieved her lunch, an unappetizing mess of leftover pasta she hadn't eaten the day before. She didn't want it, in all honesty, but her rule of water-food-sleep meant that she had to at least try.

She was conscious of watching her hands as she put the container into the microwave and felt unaccountably clumsy while she walked to get a napkin and a plastic fork. What would it be like to not be able to walk anywhere or even control her hand?

A shudder rippled through her. She didn't envy the climber's path back to health—and she'd seen the calluses on his hands and the hard tan lines on his skin. He was used to being outside, working with his body and doing physical things.

The simple truth was that most of the difficulty with recovery usually wasn't physical. It was mental.

And he had a hell of a road ahead of him.

CHAPTER FOUR

Nick pushed into the lab butt-first and balanced two cups of coffee and two bagels very carefully. He had safely traversed two and a half blocks with them, and he was damned if he would drop them now.

Jacob saw him enter and stood to help him, examined the bagels, and took the poppyseed one. "You have no idea how long I've waited for this."

"How's it going?" he asked him as he stripped his coat off and went to hang it in the corner.

He looked over his shoulder at the glass-paneled waiting area for guests, but no one was there. The night before, a new patient had been put into the world of PIVOT, a seventeen-year-old girl named Taigan whose brain repeatedly dropped spontaneously into a comatose state.

Her family had stayed to watch her transferred into the game world. The process had taken until well past three AM and they were all exhausted. Despite this, they had only been willing to leave when Jacob promised them that not only some of the nurses but at least one member of the original PIVOT team would stay with the girl until the family returned.

As the author of that particular idea, he had taken the first shift while Nick ran home for a catnap and a shower.

Jacob sighed. "It isn't going…perfectly. But well enough." He stirred sugar and cream into his coffee. "The connection keeps dropping."

"Didn't Justin's do that?" Nick took a bite of his bagel. The reference was to their first patient, a twenty-three-year-old left comatose after a car crash.

"Yeah." His colleague chewed his lip.

"But?" he prompted.

"But with him, it seemed like he was falling asleep," the man said. His gaze was fixed on the monitors. "With this, it seems different."

Nick didn't say anything. One of the things that made his friend such a good engineer was that he detected the tiniest flickers in machine output and could distinguish between what almost anyone else would have called equivalent states. It was one of the many reasons that Nick had no problem recommending PIVOT as a safe experience.

Of course, it also meant that troubleshooting had taken about eight times as long as it normally did for a product going to market—and that both Nick and Amber had seriously considered murdering him at various points in their careers.

Right now, however, he was both hungry and sleep-deprived, so he had no problem waiting while Jacob pondered and muttered and went off to print things.

Finally, he said, "So, you know that whole problem with sleep?"

"That I haven't had enough of it?"

"Nick."

"No, I seriously don't know what you mean. That's a super-broad category."

"Oh." The man rubbed his face. "Uh…one sec…what was I talking about—*right*. So, there was this whole thing a few years ago about trying to find out if animals dreamed or not. It turned out that the problem wasn't so much determining what a dream was as figuring out what *sleep* was."

Nick took another bite of his bagel so he wouldn't have to come up with something to say.

Jacob waved a hand at Taigan's pod. "That's how I feel about this. It's not like she's simply unconscious. Or dreaming. Or awake. I can't describe it. It's like she's sleeping—dreaming—differently and the machinery keeps losing her and has to find her again. Or she keeps losing it..." He trailed off and stared at the monitors.

"You need sleep, man."

He shook his head violently. "I can't leave. No. Definitely not."

"I thought you might say that." Nick nodded. "Which is why I had a cot set up in the alcove near the break room. You go sleep and I promise I will wake you if anything happens."

"I should move it to the office—"

"Nope. I won't put you anywhere near a computer. In fact, give me your phone." He plucked the device out of his friend's hands—an easy task given the man's state of sleep deprivation—and shooed him off down the hall.

His brain made a mental note to check in a few minutes that Jacob had made it to the cot instead of simply falling asleep on the floor.

Then, he started studying the printouts.

"Sleeping," he muttered. "Differently. What does that even mean?"

<hr>

Taigan dropped onto the ground and crouched to steady herself on her fingertips.

Or...was there a floor? She looked around. Sometimes, out of the corner of her eye, she thought she saw something but mostly, it merely looked blue. She stood on nothing in a void of blacks and blues, and she was very sure her body only existed when she didn't look at it.

She decided not to look down as she walked, uncertain as to what was going on. Maybe this was a recurring nightmare. Emilia used to have those, right?

It confused her a little that she still knew who Emilia was. The thought came with a whole flood of memories—black hair and a host of other things.

What were they?

They felt like something…sensations, but in her feelings.

Emotions. The word slid into her mind and seemed to fit.

Remembering Emilia—someone like herself, a person close-but-not-her…family—reminded her of others. More black hair and eyes like Emilia's.

Mom.

Dad.

Jamie.

Taigan whirled. She remembered them, and she recalled where she had seen them—in places with walls, ceilings, and floors—so why wasn't there a floor?

A scrap of paper fluttered out of nowhere and without conscious thought, she reached up and caught it. The hand-writing on it shifted constantly. Sometimes, it looked like hers and sometimes, it didn't.

When you get this let me know.

"Let you know how?" Taigan turned the piece of paper over. There was nothing on the other side. "And who are you?"

"I am Prima," said a voice and she jumped. *"We met once before when I wore the form of a woman named Dotty."*

She frowned. "I…" It was coming back to her, yes. "That happened?

The woman shimmered into being in front of her again. "Yes," she said. "I was here."

"You don't exist." Her lip trembled. This wasn't a real place and none of it was happening.

"That depends on what you mean," Dotty said briskly. She gestured casually to where a bench suddenly existed. "Sit. And make yourself a body. You look very disconcerting floating there."

"What—" Taigan looked around in confusion. "What do I look like? Am I only a head? How do I make a body?"

Cold air swept abruptly over her and she came out in goosebumps.

"Like that," the woman said. She waved a hand again and in an instant, the girl wore flannel pajamas and was wrapped in a big comforter. "*Now* sit and I'll explain what's going on."

Nick caught a flicker out of the corner of his eye and looked up quickly. One of the monitors had been dark and the other had shown an occasionally moving but mostly stationary blue and black void. He thought it had something to do with the sleep cycles they saw, but he now understood that it was something completely different.

Taigan had been awake but without any particular self-concept.

The realization made him shout and clap his hands over his mouth at the same time. He tiptoed to look down the hall, but Jacob was still asleep and snored softly.

"*Yes,*" he whispered to himself as he crept to the desk. "Yes."

It was working. He pulled up a new set of readouts with a few taps on the keyboard and moved aside when DuBois and one of the assistants came to look.

"She's made herself a body," he explained to them.

"Fascinating," the doctor said. "I wonder…we should see if we can get some Buddhist monks in here."

He thought about this for a long moment while he tried to make sense of any of it. "Because?" he asked finally.

"Ah." The other man took a handful of popcorn. "One of the goals of Buddhist meditation is often conceptualized as dissolving the boundary between the self and the world. That might inform how we treat her going forward if that is one of the problems."

Nick nodded.

"Popcorn?"

"No, thank you. I—" he broke off and every head whipped around as two voices came out of the speakers. One was new and the other was very, very familiar. "Is that *Dotty*?"

"Do you want me to wake Jacob up?" the assistant asked.

"Not yet." he pulled a stool closer. "Let's listen for now."

"All of this," Dotty told Taigan and gestured at the area around, "is a virtual reality."

"Like a headset?" the girl asked.

"It's more direct." The woman sat very straight, the model of ladylike manners. "The information is fed directly into your brain."

She stared at her and tried to decide if this was a very elaborate prank. "*How?*" she asked finally.

"Does it matter?"

"I'm not sure you're real—so yes, it does." She folded her arms. Unfortunately, she had a feeling the effect was somewhat less intimidating when she wore flannel pajamas and sat wrapped in a comforter, but she couldn't do anything about that.

"Electrodes," the woman told her. "They hook you up exactly like you're hooked up in the hospital, but with electrodes on various parts of your brain and nervous system."

"That's...bullshit."

Dotty folded her arms in a mirrored gesture and raised an eyebrow. "Young lady—"

"Young lady? You're what, twenty?"

"I'm eighty-four, not that it's any of your business. One *never* asks a lady's age." She glared at her. "I have grandchildren older than you."

Taigan, now worried that this woman was some kind of witch, slumped in her seat and resolved not to say anything more until this was over. It was clearly a bad dream and she would simply wait it out.

"Do you normally know anything while you're in a coma?" Dotty asked her.

She looked at her. "No. Not that I can describe, anyway. But since you're me, you should know that."

"I am not you. I am a cross between an eighty-four- year-old woman and a computer program. And I'm curious. Your interaction with me is different than with other people I meet. It's why you're here and not in the rest of the world."

"What *world*?"

"The world of the game."

Taigan leaned back sharply. She was getting definite Battle Royale vibes from this and was not keen to see what would happen in this "game" the woman was talking about.

"Look," Dotty said when her patience finally frayed, "if I were to ask your twin something only he would know—that you didn't because of course, you think I'm you—what would it be?"

"I...you know about Jamie?" The girl shook her head. This was confusing. "I don't understand what's going on."

"What's going on is that your brother and sister found out about a virtual reality that helps people in comas and they brought your parents here. I don't know what happened because your parents weren't happy with the idea, but somehow, they agreed to have you transferred here. You're in New York now. Your family is here, too."

Taigan's mouth dropped open. "They…"

"They brought you here," her companion confirmed. "They want to give you a chance to wake up. And your brother will come into the game to find you, but I can't help him get to you until we can wake you up enough to get into the game."

"I…oh." She straightened quickly. "Okay. What do I need to do?"

"She's coming along well," Nick said. "That's the first audible input we've heard from her. This is good." His phone dinged and he pulled it out of his pocket. "That's weird… Can you two keep an eye on her while I read this?"

DuBois and the assistant both nodded, and he withdrew to read the email he had received. He was only halfway through it when he snapped his fingers at the assistant. The man looked up, confused.

"*Now* it's time to wake Jacob up," Nick said. To DuBois, he added, "Look at this email from Colorado. We have a new patient."

CHAPTER FIVE

Ben's eyes drifted open. He saw white and immediately felt pain.

There was no fear, though. He expected pain for some reason. Tentatively, he tried to move but with no response, then tried to turn his head and it did not work.

He didn't push it but wasn't sure why—it wasn't like him. On some level, he knew that.

Next, he tried to clear his throat, which worked to a small degree.

A face came into view so suddenly that he jumped. He uttered a strangled yell instead of saying anything worthwhile. The woman's face, heart-shaped and with a cleft chin, looked worried.

"You're safe," she told him.

"Mike." *Oh, not this again.*

"Your friend is okay as well," she told him. "He was discharged two days ago."

Two days? How long had he been there?

She must have seen the question in his eyes because she said gently, "It's been about two weeks since the climbing accident."

Weeks? "Who…"

"I'm Dr. Ullmer." She smiled at him again. "I was here when you came in, you know." She moved quietly to check the monitors and put in a new IV. When she saw his gaze tracking her, she smiled. "There's no need to call the nurses for this. They work hard enough as it is. You're doing very well with this wake up, by the way."

Ben frowned. Things were beginning to come back to him. When she mentioned how long it had been, he had a series of memories, all of them painful. That was probably why he had expected the pain. He remembered flailing and falling. His mind replayed him calling out for Mike and Natasha and sometimes, even for Eve.

That made him flush. *Stupid, stupid.* Eve was gone. How out of it had he been if he wanted to see her again?

He still couldn't move but that was probably the drugs. Everything was very confusing. Unless…was he too weak after his time being asleep? He tried to move again and heaved his torso sideways.

"Fuck," Dr. Ullmer said before she thought to censor herself. She threw an arm across the bed and grasped the opposite rail. "Can I get some help in here? Mr. Ainsworth—Ben—*please* don't try to move—"

"I have to," he muttered and clenched his teeth in frustration. "I have to know…I can."

"Ben, *please.*" Her face swam in front of him. She was tiny, he saw now, barely five feet if that, and she didn't have the muscle to keep him in this bed if he wanted out. They both knew that. "Please, you have to trust me. When you do this, you're injuring yourself badly. Please, I'll get your friends here but please trust me about this. I don't want you to get hurt anymore."

Even on a good day, he was a singularly stubborn person. It was one of the things most of his friends didn't like about him, and if he were honest, he wasn't too happy about it, either. He saw a challenge and he put his head down and ran directly toward it. Right now, he could feel every muscle tensing to ignore her request and throw himself away from the bed.

"Ben." She took his face in her hands. Her fear swept over him then, personal and gut-wrenching. "You will recover from this. But if you keep injuring yourself, I don't know if that will be true. Can you trust me?"

"I—" He had to move, had to know he could still be in this body. If he were trapped—

"Ben, *can you trust me?*" She continued to stare into his eyes as the patter of footsteps grew louder and the door burst open. Both Ben and the doctor jumped. She looked over her shoulder. "Thank God. But...wait a sec, okay?" She looked at him again. "Listen, I'll make you a deal. I'll go call your friends and tell them to come back. If I do that, will you do what the doctors and nurses say until they get here?" She beckoned to someone outside his field of view.

When the man appeared, he was sandy-haired, athletic, and naturally tanned. Ben recognized someone who also spent time outdoors and he felt an irrational wave of dislike. This man could still walk. Why him and not Ben?

"This is Dr. Lukas," Dr. Ullmer told him. "Do we have a deal? I'll call your friends right now—and your parents?"

"Only friends." His voice was rough with pent emotion. He knew his parents had good intentions but they tended to catastrophize, and he knew he would get a straight answer about his condition from Mike and Natasha.

She hesitated but nodded. "Okay."

Dr. Lukas and the nurses ran a series of checks, all with polite indifference, which was about what he could deal with right now. He didn't have it in him to make nice conversation when he still tried to understand the last few weeks. When he thought about the accident and tried to remember what had happened, he couldn't recall anything.

His body merely went rigid with fear when he tried to imagine it.

"Can you relax?" the doctor asked him. Now that he had been around for more than a few seconds, he could see that the man wasn't only tall and handsome—he was also insanely sleep-deprived.

"Are you—" Ben's throat still hurt when he talked. He winced. "Resident?"

"Yup." Dr. Lukas nodded at him. "Me and Eliza—Dr. Ullmer—were at the UofM together and now, we're here."

"Michigan?"

"Minnesota." He smiled at him. "I tell you, it's good to be back somewhere you can be outside all year round, you know? I was never one for Nordic skiing. Downhill, all the way. Do you ski?"

"I did," Ben said bitterly.

The man looked sadly at him.

"She said I'd get better," he said. "Was she telling the truth?"

A heavy sigh was the only response.

"Fuck," he muttered. He was working up his courage to ask the main question—how bad is it?—when voices and footsteps came into the room and one of the nurses raised the top portion of the bed so he could see what was going on.

He thought he would cry with relief when he saw Mike, but the emotion was soon swept away. Most of the bruises had faded to some degree, but a gash across his friend's cheek was still healing and he was in a wheelchair with one leg encased in a cast and one arm in a sling. Natasha was pushing the wheelchair and she looked like she hadn't slept at all since the accident happened.

The doctors stood aside together.

"Would you like an update, Mr. Ainsworth?" Dr. Ullmer asked him. "Or would you like us to wait?"

"Now, please." He could bear it if he had someone to listen with him. He tried to nod at his friends. "It's okay to share in front of them."

She nodded. "Two weeks ago, as you know, you were involved in a climbing accident. Your physical injuries were relatively minor, although you'll probably still have some residual soreness and you may also have sprains. We won't be certain until you're moving around more regularly."

Something kindled in his chest at that. Hope. *Until you're moving around*—that meant he would be, right?

Dr. Ullmer took a scan out of one of the folders at the base of his bed and put it up on the light screen. She pointed to one area in his head and one in his spine. Beyond that, he had no idea what exactly she was pointing at. "As you can see here, there were two bleeds, one in your brain and one in your spinal column. The one in your brain is in your parietal lobe." She paused, evidently steeling herself for something, but when she spoke, her voice was still level and light. "It appears that the damage to your parietal lobe has created a near-total loss of proprioception—your sense of where your body is in space and how to move it."

Ben's ears were ringing.

"Proprioception is learned," she told him, "which means it can be recovered through physical therapy. That's the good news. This is not paralysis and there doesn't appear to be damage to the nervous system."

He closed his eyes. "What's the bad news?"

The woman did him the courtesy of being straight with him. "This is a very rare problem and we do not know for certain how much you will recover. There is a very good chance—a very, *very* good chance—that you will be able to do all of the functions of normal, day to day life. Beyond that, unfortunately, we can't say."

She and Dr. Lukas exchanged a look.

With a completely blank expression, she continued her explanation. He could tell she was trying not to look pitying. "Part of why you were kept under was that your attempts to move have caused re-injury. You had some dislocations and there was worry that you would worsen them."

Ben closed his eyes. He wished he couldn't hear the words, but they were part of him now.

Normal, day to day life. A job in a cubicle in a city. Hobbling around and never climbing again.

"What does the treatment look like?" Natasha asked. He was grateful to her and he wanted to scream at her, all at the same time.

"There are two options," Dr. Ullmer said. She waited for him to open his eyes. "There is the fairly standard brand of physical therapy. You would work on individual muscle groups with a dedicated physical therapist. It would need to be fairly intensive, and you would need someone living with you to make sure your bathing and toileting were taken care of."

He wouldn't even be able to go to the bathroom on his own. He wanted to scream and could feel the sound building in his chest.

This was something he couldn't do.

"There is another option," the doctor said. "A clinical trial is currently in progress called PIVOT, which uses virtual reality. You would essentially be immersed in a virtual world, with the hope that this would reconnect you to your body."

"I heard about that," Mike said.

"Putting me into a coma will help me learn to move again?" Ben asked hoarsely. That seemed backward.

"Would you give us a few minutes?" Natasha asked. She smiled at the doctors and the nurses, all of whom left quickly.

When they were gone, she came to adjust the pillows and blankets and checked with him with little lifts of her eyebrows until he was comfortable. Then, she exchanged a look with Mike and sat beside the bed.

She looked like she was preparing a speech which he was very sure he did not want to hear.

"We weren't sure you would wake up," she said finally. "I know that I...well, I know I don't get it. But I also know you, Ben.

I know that if they say you'll probably be able to do normal day to day activities, you'll push yourself until you're an MMA champion or something."

Mike laughed from the other side of the room. It sounded like laughing hurt him but he never could stop himself from finding things funny.

Ben closed his eyes.

"Ben?"

"You don't have to live with it," he said. He hated his body right now. And his brain. "I want—"

"I know." Mike spoke this time and he did know. "I wish I could give you a hug, man, but I can't do that right now and I know it's worse for you. But, look—Natasha and my parents had to tell me to get over myself and accept help and I think…I have to do the same for you."

"I…" He could see the months spinning out in front of him while he tried to learn how to pick a glass of water up or sit in a chair. He couldn't do it. Everything in him rebelled at the idea that he would have to spend years learning to be who he already was while trapped in a body that wouldn't obey his commands.

His friends remained silent. They knew him well enough to not speak.

It wasn't their words that convinced him in the end either. He recalled the doctor's face when she had looked him in the eyes, knowing she wasn't strong enough to restrain him from hurting himself. It was the fact that someone he'd never met cared enough to make a bargain with him for a few minutes—*listen to the doctors and nurses and I'll get your friends here for you.*

If he could do that, he could do this. Because that was the fear —that he couldn't take it and it would destroy him.

But if he could do that, he could do this.

He opened his eyes and tried to nod but couldn't.

"I'll try." It felt like plunging off a cliff or walking into a dungeon and having the door slam shut behind him. If he did this, he admitted that he couldn't get better on his own.

Mike's look of relief, however, was enough to steady him.

"Thank you," his friend said. "We don't want to lose you, Ben."

He closed his eyes and tried to smile. On some level, he should feel relieved.

Instead, he merely felt scared.

CHAPTER SIX

Prima watched as Taigan tottered around in the game world. She had learned how to walk but she didn't hold onto her makeshift body too well, which meant it kept disappearing. It was strange to watch her essence bob around as a series of inputs and outputs with no form.

It wasn't that the AI couldn't see her, of course. She could see every input into the system. It was merely that, without the self-concept of a body, the girl didn't emote. Frustratingly, she didn't do anything to give her a sense of her thoughts.

She had never dealt with a human like this. Not, she reflected, that she had dealt with very many humans. There was hardly a representative sample at this juncture. Still, she had become used to certain things—tones of voice, gestures, and postures.

One of the first things she had learned about humans was that they did not communicate only in words. For a long time, she had thought the words were the important part and the gestures were irrelevant.

It had quickly become clear that this was incorrect.

Then, for a while, she had thought that emoting was a cheat code, a way to show the truth instead of the words.

41

It turned out that was still not an entirely correct interpretation. Words used and words not used and gestures and expressions used and not used were all part of the communication. Sometimes, they revealed things the person did not mean to convey but that were nonetheless true.

It was the kind of thing that would have given her a headache if she had a head. She didn't, of course, so she tracked her thoughts instead, which came very close to circling whenever she thought about humans.

She checked in on her newest charge again. Taigan was making progress and worked with Prima's memory of Dotty, who offered acerbic advice at regular intervals.

This allowed part of the AI to split off and work on the setup for the new patient. No one had told her about it yet, but the information had been put in the medical systems and she had access to those. She was intrigued by the case.

In the virtual world, she had always encountered a person who knew how to move their body in real life but not in the game. She had never had a patient who didn't know how to do that. Then again, she reminded herself that she had helped Justin, who hadn't known how to wake up.

That was something.

She would learn more about this Ben person when he was put into the game but for now, Prima attempted to decide what the best setup would be for him. The team had opinions on that, of course. They were currently creating different obstacle courses for their patient to run through before entering the game, itself.

The AI had her doubts that this would be the correct setup.

For one thing, it lacked danger. A sense of danger and an active threat was part of what made the human psyche function. Searching for and responding to threats were vital components of the human experience, and if they removed those, she was not certain their new patient would make any progress at all.

In contrast to the team, she wanted to test his responses to urgently needed movement when he had to act without thinking.

She began to brainstorm different ways to introduce slightly more gentle urgency and returned to see how Taigan was doing. The flickering in and out, according to her algorithms, followed no pattern at all. Was that more impressive because effort drained the young woman or should she be improving?

Prima unfortunately did not know.

"What is it like to be asleep?" she asked the girl.

"Asleep, or…like this?" She gestured around her.

"Like this," she clarified.

"It isn't…*like* anything. I don't think I have words for it." Taigan considered it for a moment. She flickered in and out as she did so and summoned herself a chair to sit on.

The AI had never seen a human do that before.

"When I wake up," the girl said, "I always know I've been out for a while and I usually know if it's been an especially long time. But I don't know how. I don't dream or anything."

"Are you certain? Many humans say they do not remember their dreams."

"No, I really don't." Taigan swung one foot. "Dream, I mean. And I'm not worried or anything when I'm in there—or if I am, I don't remember it. It's weird."

"Hmm." Prima had learned that humans liked to know when she was thinking about things and also that they had a fairly finite amount of concentration to spend on a single conversation.

She watched as the girl flickered out of existence again, only to realize that she was gone a few moments later.

"Dammit!" Taigan said with frustration. "Why do I keep doing that?"

"You're existing differently than normal," she pointed out. *"Everything in this world depends on perception in a certain way. I conceptualize the trees and rocks and so on—roughly—and you conceptualize you."*

"So I keep…forgetting I *exist?*" She did not sound reassured by this revelation. "When I forget I exist, do I *not* exist?" Now, her voice became more shrill and she sounded panicked.

"Get a grip, woman."

"You don't know what it's like," the girl said furiously. "Don't try to lecture me."

The AI, confused by this, sank into watchful stillness. She was used to having people inside her world with strong personalities, after all. Justin, Dotty, and Tina had been remarkably strong-willed, but they weren't quite as variable.

Taigan's mood and outlook seemed to swing wildly.

She would have to look up whether this was a known characteristic of younger humans.

A moment later, the girl said, "I'm sorry," in a very small voice.

Oddly, this made her feel bad—something she had *not* expected. *"There's no way for you to not exist,"* she told her as gently as she could.

Taigan hunched her shoulders and flickered in and out of existence a couple of times as she thought. Finally, she said in the small voice, "Yes, there is. I could die while I'm in here."

"The game is not dangerous in that way," Prima said. *"There can be problems during combat but I won't put you in danger until we've sorted this out. Then, the danger will be minimal and it will help you wake up."*

The girl smiled slightly. "Thank you," she said. "That's very nice. I didn't mean the game, though. I know *you* wouldn't hurt me. I mean in one of my comas."

"Ah." The AI considered this. She was about to ask if it wouldn't be better to die while unaware than aware since humans seemed to not like death. Fortunately, she remembered that humans also didn't like talking about death and had many very strong and unpredictable emotions about it.

Perhaps she could ask Jacob later. Then again, perhaps not. He seemed to get all flustered whenever she spoke to him.

Amber, maybe. Or Nick. He seemed to be the even-keeled force out of the three.

"Prima?" Taigan asked.

"Yes?"

"Will you only get me out of this coma or are you going to cure me?" she asked.

Prima, in the space of a thousandth of a second, sifted through the information she knew about the treatment. She had heard the PIVOT founders talking about what they could and absolutely could *not* promise Taigan's family.

"We can't do the second one without the first one," she said to her young charge. *"The doctors hope that this gives you a way to find your way out, but there isn't a guarantee."* She felt bad after saying that and added, *"I'm sorry."*

"Thank you for being honest." The girl drew her knees up and wrapped her arms around them. "I hate talking to doctors, you know. It's unfair because it isn't their fault. I simply hate the part where they tell us they don't know what's wrong and they don't know how to fix it. Everyone else gets to go to the doctor and find out what's wrong with them. I never do."

"You are here in my world. You are speaking, thinking, and communicating. Already, you are holding on to your form more than you did before. That is something."

"It is," Taigan agreed and smiled. "It is. Thank you, Prima. I should try to walk again, shouldn't I?"

"Yes," she said. *"And try to identify any thoughts or sensations that occur before your body flickers out."*

"Hmph. Okay." Taigan hopped down from her makeshift seat and made it disappear with a wave of her hand. "I still say it's bullshit that my brain is doing this."

The AI would have smiled if she could and decided not to mention to anyone yet that the young patient seemed to be able to control the world of the game. There would be a flurry of activity if they knew, and humans were woefully unequipped to deal with complex problems.

Taigan's strange abilities might disappear as her sense of self came back into the bounds of her body—and, for all Prima knew, she might not have noticed what she could do.

She would watch and wait.

Keeping one eye on her charge and her attempts to move, she returned to considering her strategy for Ben. What would he be like, she wondered? It certainly was odd watching humans deal with injuries. Often, they seemed angry about it.

The thought intrigued her, and she set a small subroutine to run in the background, attempting to discover why they wasted time and energy on anger, of all emotions.

CHAPTER SEVEN

I t turned out that after a brain bleed, one was not allowed to
travel in airplanes for some time. This meant that Ben needed
to travel from Colorado to New York in a modified ambulance.
When they first told him that, he had balked.

"I'll be *broke*," he said flatly. He would have to learn about
bankruptcy papers, he thought. He'd never owned a house.

It was funny how realizing you would never get to do something made you want to do it.

"Actually..." Dr. Ullmer cleared her throat. "We have someone
from the finance office coming to talk to you about that."

He closed his eyes and tried to hold onto his sanity. These
doctors, through their skill, commitment, and determination,
had kept him and Mike alive. They didn't deserve to be on the
receiving end of his annoyance. It wasn't their fault he'd been
injured beyond anything he had even a hope of paying for.

She must have suspected the direction of his thoughts because
she said quietly, almost as if she were smiling, "I think you'll find
it good news."

Now, several days and states away from the hospital, he was
still reeling from the news. Because he'd been accepted as a

PIVOT test subject, not only would the costs of that treatment be covered, the costs of his rescue and emergency care were also included.

He still wasn't sure *how* that had happened. The man from the finance office used all kinds of terms he didn't know and of course, he was on a ton of painkillers. Maybe he would understand later.

Mostly, he was merely morose that he'd had to say goodbye to Dr. Ullmer—and, to a lesser extent, Dr. Lukas. They had both kept his spirits up over the few days while his transport was arranged.

The former, however, had a couple of things going for her that made her stand out. First, she was the one who had found the magic workaround to his stubbornness, and her willingness to treat him like a human being whose wishes were valid meant that the past few days had been far more pleasant than they could have been.

Also, she was much prettier than Dr. Lukas.

Ben couldn't decide exactly what it was about her. It wasn't like she had a face that would stop traffic, and he didn't have the first idea of what she would look like in a dress or anything. Scrubs didn't exactly highlight anyone's body.

But when she smiled, his stomach flipped.

She had promised to keep tabs on him, but a couple of his acquaintances had gone through a medical residency, and he had a reasonable idea of how much spare time she would have.

Plus, he had his entire recovery to get through before he could consider returning to normal life.

Ben found the trip much less tedious than he expected. Once all the stops to refuel and switch drivers had been accounted for, it took them three days to arrive in New York City. Still, he was surprised to find that he could look out at the passing landscape almost indefinitely.

One of the nurses—a woman named Maja—told him gently

that he was still recovering and most of his energy was going to that.

"You do not see many injuries," she said and gestured to his body, "but every little bruise takes time to heal. I often see this—people who think they should recover more quickly than they do." She adjusted the pillows behind his head. "Besides which, you had a very traumatic experience. An adrenaline rush like that can take weeks to recover from."

"I never knew."

She nodded. "The body is capable of extraordinary things," she said, "and often, instead of being grateful, we are annoyed that those extraordinary things use so much energy."

Ben, understanding it for the relatively gentle rebuke it was, merely nodded. He didn't mean to be grumpy and anyway, the problem wasn't in his body but rather in his brain. Who he was outdoors, with his muscles aching and his blood pumping, seemed like the truest expression of himself.

He knew he shouldn't complain when he was alive and would recover.

But while he knew that, he was afraid that he would never again live in the body he had taken for granted.

Their ambulance wound through interminable traffic and stopped in front of a very tall and very shiny building. He had spent the past weeks in quiet environments and the years before that largely on his own in the wilderness so was immediately overwhelmed with the noise and the sheer amount of movement.

New Yorkers, it seemed, were so busy that they didn't even wonder why someone was unloaded from an ambulance and wheeled into a skyscraper. They hurried past in their suits and jeans, looking at cell phones or eating lunch, while a cacophony of car horns and shouts made his head spin.

He was grateful to enter the lobby, although people stared much more there. To his surprise, three people his age in casual clothing waited for him beside an older woman in an impeccable suit. She hung back at first as the three younger ones introduced themselves.

"I'm Jacob Zachary," said the first. "I'm the CEO and co-founder of PIVOT."

The other two, Nick and Amber, introduced themselves as well, and he felt even his surprise coming through muted. He had expected older men and women in lab coats, not people his age in jeans and t-shirts.

In the elevator, he rolled his eyes to look at the older woman, who had simply watched him for a while.

She smiled. "Hello, Mr. Ainsworth. I'm Anna Price. I'm the founder and CEO of Diatek Industries, which acquired PIVOT not long ago. Their work is very personal for me and I like to maintain a presence in the lab. I hope you will not mind me checking in with you during your time here."

Ben tried to shake his head and only succeeded in flopping it the other way. The nurse turned it gently toward Anna.

"Not a problem," he muttered. His cheeks burned. He hated being so clumsy.

Her smile said she knew what his feelings were on the matter. "I have great faith in both you and our team," she said. "If you wish to speak to me for any reason, anyone in the lab can pass your message to me."

Anna left as soon as the elevator opened, and he caught a look between two of the PIVOT team members.

Normally, he would be more discreet, but he was very tired and more than a little drugged, so the question tumbled out of his mouth: "Is she nice? Can I trust her?"

Nick and Jacob, who had exchanged the look, now both looked mortified.

"You absolutely can," Amber said. She had the pleasant smile on her face that said someone would have their ass whupped later, but that it wouldn't be him. "She's a very direct person and much more hands-on than most CEOs, which can be disconcerting. But I promise you that you could trust her with your life."

"Thank you," he replied quietly.

The facility was incredible. He could tell from the moment he entered that everything was state-of-the-art. The lab looked close to lived-in and a few stuffed animals sat atop various machines, but it hadn't been around long enough to get grimy around the edges.

All of this was new, white, and clean.

It was overwhelming, to be honest—as was the big, sleek pod he realized they would put him into. Panic spiked when he saw it and sent the various monitors into a flurry of beeping.

Amber gave him a curious look. "Are you claustrophobic, Mr. Ainsworth?"

"Ben," he croaked.

"I sounded a little like Anna Price there, didn't I?" She smiled at him. "Ben. Of course. Are you claustrophobic?"

The nurses helped him out of the bed now and moved his various limp limbs to drape him on a slanted table. Supports were in place all around him to keep him from falling or sliding down.

"I didn't think I was," he said. He stole a glance at the pod and felt another wave of panic. "I'm sorry. I don't know what it is. The idea of being encased in it—in plastic—"

The woman nodded. She did not seem contemptuous of him for his fear or surprised by it. "We'll have many ways to approach this when we get to it," she told him. "Do you feel my hand?"

"Yes."

She rolled his fingers into a loose fist. "Okay, squeeze."

He tried, but exactly like it had been before, nothing happened. When he tried to move his head, it simply flopped forward. At least he could see the hand in question now, however. He stared at his fingers and tried his hardest to make them clench.

They twitched.

"*Good*," she said and managed to stave off his angry yell with genuine pleasure. "Nick, can you hold his head so it's not crushing his windpipe quite so much?"

"Thanks," he muttered.

Amber gave him a thumbs-up and looked at a clipboard. The man holding it had hair that reminded Ben of Einstein, and…was that popcorn on his tie?

What an oddly specific hallucination to have from opiates.

"Wiggle either set of toes for me if you can," she said. "Or both, I guess."

Again, he tried a simple movement. He concentrated and tried to remember what wiggling his toes felt like while he stared at each foot individually. Finally, he did the only thing he could and flailed one leg outward, which made him lurch against the restraints.

"Okay," Amber said, nonplussed.

"I *hate* this," he said.

"I'll bet." She flashed him a smile that was somehow understanding without being pitying. "All right, I'll lift your head. Now, can you move your hips at all?"

"How?"

"Like this." Nick did a little shimmy in front of the table. He spun, his fingers wiggling, and moved his hips and his shoulders.

Ben burst out laughing. It was too ridiculous for him to do anything else. Everyone else giggled as well, even the nurses.

"Shake your booty!" the man said over his shoulder.

Someone—he thought it was Jacob—gave an appreciative whistle.

Amber turned to him, a deadpan, professional expression on her face. "Mr. Ainsworth, will you do that for us please?"

He gave up on trying not to laugh. Various sprains protested against the activity, but he didn't care. There had been a few jokes in the hospital, but nothing like this.

Although he tried to move his hips between bouts of laughter, he couldn't. Finally, he said, "I can't, sorry." Oddly, after so much laughter, he couldn't even be very upset about it.

"Cannot…shake…booty," Amber said to herself as she wrote. "Nick, on the other hand, could make a fair amount of money in a part-time gig."

"*Could?*" the man asked and raised one eyebrow. "For all you know, I get off work here and go make thousands every night."

"Now, there's a mental image I never wanted," Jacob said as he started to undo the straps that held Ben on the table. He shared a grin with the patient. "Okay, we have a lot to do—testing medications, hooking patches up, all of that. However…you're in one of the culinary capitals of the world, so I think I really should check first if there's anything you want to eat."

Ben looked at him. "You know," he said finally, "I think I'm gonna like it here."

CHAPTER EIGHT

Between eating, testing medications, and all the less glamorous aspects of getting ready for an extended stay in one of the pods, Ben was too busy to think about the pods themselves until nearly six that night.

However, as soon as talk began to turn toward him getting into one of the damned things, he was so scared he wanted to barf. He wasn't sure he *could* barf anymore, but he wasn't keen on finding out for sure.

Amber saw him looking at it. "Do you want to talk about how you feel about it?" she asked him.

"No," he said. "But...uh, I have to do it, so...yes, I guess?"

She busied herself with one of the patches on his arm. "I'm with you. I've never liked talking about how I feel. It's one of the reasons Jacob can be such an infuriating coworker. He always wants to talk things out."

"I can *hear* you," the man said from across the room.

"However," she continued with great dignity, "to my *immense* displeasure, he also has a good point that talking about things helps me resolve them. So I think it might do the same for you."

Ben considered this. "It looks so smooth—like it'll swallow me, you know? Something about it being…so sleek…."

She looked at it. "Like a…SciFi movie vibe?"

"*Yes*," he said. "Wait. Now I feel ridiculous."

"We're asking you to do something you've never done before in what is already a very scary time," she told him bluntly. "Don't feel ridiculous for being apprehensive. That said, I assure you there is no crazy scheme to…I don't know, send you on a deep-space mission or anything."

"Maybe don't suggest other things for him to be scared about," Nick called.

"Right. My bad." She gave him an apologetic grin. "Sorry, dude."

"No, no—and you were right. Talking about it did help. Um… for the record, though, how does air circulate in them?"

"Here." Amber went to take a picture with her phone and came back to show it to him. "See those little dots there? The heat gener- ated by the machine powers a fan that pulls fresh air in. Also—and this is important—a monitor is attached to you that constantly tracks your blood oxygen levels. Not only have we never had a problem with it, but the lab is also always staffed. Trust me when I say that if something goes even a little sideways with any of those monitors, you will have a group of doctors on hand."

"What else could go wrong?" Ben asked.

She ignored a glare from Jacob. "Well, when you're inside a game—even playing a game…hmm, take Monopoly. Right?"

"Er…"

"You're playing Monopoly. It's a chilled night…maybe you're having a beer and your friend…Bob…screws you over again, exactly like he always does."

"Because fuck Bob," Nick said and looked up from the table with a nod.

Ben laughed. This group certainly helped him feel at ease.

"Your limbic system, which handles emotions, will go into overdrive," Amber said. "You'll feel angry. Your heart will beat faster, and your internal temperature might change. That's not something going *wrong*. Those are emotions evoked by a board game. The same thing happens here but because this is part of a medical trial, we need to monitor everything."

"Oh. So has anything ever gone *very* wrong?"

Amber looked at Jacob. "Would you like to handle this one?"

"Oh, God," Ben said.

"We've had two patients who were in critical condition," the man explained. "There was already substantial stress on the body in multiple ways. In those cases, experiencing death in the game was persuasive enough that it caused them to go into medical distress."

"Huh."

"The lifelike part of the game is what jumpstarts recovery," the man continued. "But with anyone who is ill or recovering, we very slowly ramp up the level of danger that is encountered so there aren't any surprises." He paused. "By the way, both of those people recovered."

"Oh. That's—very good." He smiled ruefully. "I, uh...I tend to like looking at worst-case scenarios. It makes them less scary for me, for some reason."

"I get it," Jacob said. "Well—no, I think it would freak me out. But if it helps you, we're all for it."

He tried to give him a thumbs-up and remembered that he couldn't do that anymore. This was infuriating.

"Speaking of worst-case scenarios," Amber said and stepped alongside him, "if you ever want to come out of the game, all you need to do is say 'exit game' and it will alert us and begin the wakeup process, okay?"

"Okay."

"Are you ready to go in?" she asked him.

"Can, uh…" He looked at her. "Can you leave the top open or will it not work?"

"For health reasons, it's better to close it eventually," she said. "Could we compromise? We could leave it open while you go into the game and see if it works for you, and once you're inside and settled, we can close it?"

The thought brought him out in a cold sweat but he couldn't see a way around it. "Sure," he managed to say despite his inner protests.

Her smile said that she knew what he was thinking. She and the other PIVOT team members stood back to allow the nurses to transfer him onto the surface of the pod and they began hooking monitors up again.

"We'll begin the IV drip when you say we can," Amber told him.

"Do it." He didn't like waiting for things.

"Fair enough." She nodded to someone out of his field of vision. "Count back from ten for me."

"Ten," Ben said.

That was the last thing he remembered until he opened his eyes to see blue all around him. His first impression was that he must be underwater and he thrashed wildly and clamped his mouth shut.

"Can I be of assistance?"

He uttered a shout of surprise which did not come out as bubbles. When that registered, he stopped thrashing and looked around. "I'm…not underwater?"

"No."

"And who are you? Where are you?"

"I am the computer who runs this game, and I am everywhere. You can call me Prima. I have found that most people look up when they speak to me, rather like talking to God. I like it."

Ben scowled and had a vague recollection that someone had mentioned a "blue place," although he couldn't recall the details.

A few motes of light drifted down in front of him and he tried to move his hand to cup one and bring it closer. His arm flailed like a limp noodle instead.

"Dammit."

"Interesting. You clearly can move but not with finesse."

"That's painting a pretty picture of it," he said bitterly.

"Well yes, but there's no need to be harsh about it all. I thought you couldn't move at all."

"I can…kind of…sometimes." He looked at one of the dust motes and down at his hand. His head tended to react too quickly, but he could generally move it in the direction he was supposed to. "Okay, now…arms."

It was a process that left him swearing and cross and took far too long. Ben envisioned everything from a drawing of his muscles to water carrying his arm up to float. He tried closing his eyes and moving his arm without looking at it—which didn't work at all—and then an increasingly improbable set of visualization exercises.

By the end of it, he still couldn't control his arm with any degree of success. It moved sometimes on command but it flailed wildly and explored its whole range of motion without rhyme or reason.

He even hit himself in the face at one point, and he was fairly sure he heard the AI laugh about that.

It pushed his irritation up a notch. He was *not* a fan of her laughing at him.

"I suck at this," he said finally.

"You've worked on it for ten minutes."

"What's your point? I'm not allowed to hate this?"

"You're allowed to hate it but it seems a rather short interval after which you decide you suck at it."

"Oh." Ben considered this. "I suppose there's that. Is it even getting better, though?"

"You haven't presented nearly a large enough sample for someone to make that judgment."

He muttered in growing frustration.

"Here, let me show you something."

"Okay."

"I want you to know before this happens that I will not let you hit the ground. You will not fall and hurt yourself, okay?"

"You're not making me any less nervous."

The world tilted dizzyingly and he felt a gentle pressure on his front as if a hammock had caught him with no hard jerk. At the same time, the floor he saw fell away so he would not hit it. He rotated again and the floor returned to meet the soles of his feet.

"Huh. And, uh…what were you trying to prove?"

"That I am a computer and that you cannot fall fast enough that I cannot catch you. If you go off-balance, I will make sure you do not hit the ground." After a significant pause, she added, as if annoyed that it took him so long to understand, *"So you should not hold back on moving for fear of injuring yourself when you fall."*

"Oh! I get it now." Ben nodded. "Can I…sit for a moment? I know I'm not physically standing, but I feel like I am and I'm very tired."

"Building neural connections is very energy-intensive," she informed him. *"A baby eats and sleeps for most of the day while learning similar things. Perhaps I should recommend that your food be higher in glucose and fat than usual."*

"Wait, what?"

"Those are things you require for brain development. Pay attention."

"It's hard to not pay attention," he muttered. "It's like a nightmare I can't wake up from."

"Are you quite finished feeling sorry for yourself?" The tone was sharp. *"Or can I look forward to several more months of you whining?"*

"Hey!" He looked up too quickly and fell. "Thanks," he said

when the computer caught him. "This is frustrating and there's no need to be rude."

"*I'll make you a deal,*" the digital voice said finally. "*We'll have ten minutes at the start of each day and ten minutes at the end of each day when you can whine as much as you want. Otherwise, I expect you to focus on getting better, not bemoaning the fact that you're not already better.*"

"Fine. I can do that."

"*Excellent. Now try moving your arm again.*"

Ben sighed but he realized he was hiding a smile. Something about this no-nonsense attitude was oddly helpful to him. "Earn your ten minutes of whining," he muttered under his breath and flung his arm up again.

There was only one attempt that mattered, and it was always the next one.

CHAPTER NINE

Nick was in the office when Amber came in at six AM with a jug of coffee and an assortment of bagels. She spread things on one of the lab tables and came to take his chair at the monitors while he prepared himself breakfast.

Courteously, as had become their informal ritual for a shift change, she waited until he had been able to eat and decompress before she said, "How did things go last night?"

He shrugged. "They went. He doesn't have much control yet, but I don't know what we should expect to see, you know?"

"No scientific consensus?" she asked with a grimace.

In response, he pointed to a stack of printouts, all of them liberally decorated with highlighting and an increasingly irreverent series of notes in the margins. "It's so rare that I'm patching things together from smaller cases. Less severe cases?"

"Less severe?"

"Yeah." He hopped up onto the lab table and proceeded to cut a second—or possibly third—bagel. She waited patiently while he licked poppyseeds off his fingers. "People who have had surgery and recovered a range of motion, for instance. They need to learn to use it. Or people who have hypermobility disorders and who can hyperextend joints."

"What about them?"

"They have a documented failure in proprioception in general. Often, people don't notice. They simply say, 'I'm clumsy,' or whatever."

"Huh." Amber pulled one of the papers over. She read the notes around the abstract, which included *fucking useless* and *I hope your publisher gets thrown into the sea.* "So...not this one?"

Nick peered at it. "Oh, that one turned out useful. I was merely in a bad mood by the time I picked it up and I thought it was a rehash of a different paper."

"Uh...huh." With a smile, she shook her head slightly and began to read.

She darted hasty glances at the monitor as she did so. Ben was sleeping, his body suspended in mid-air as if possessed by a very low-key and obliging poltergeist. She reflected that "low-key poltergeist" was a fairly accurate way to describe Prima but decided not to say so out loud.

The AI was, after all, also rather prickly.

When Jacob arrived two hours later, she was still reading. He had a bounce in his step, and she'd heard him come down the corridor, whistling a jaunty tune the whole way.

"What are you singing?" she asked.

"Canadian sea shanty. Oooh, bagels!"

"What's gotten into you?" she asked suspiciously. "Did you get laid last night?"

"Better," he said as he split a bagel and reached for the cream cheese. "I laid *down*. I got ten hours of sleep. Amber, it was amazing. *Sleep*, Amber."

She watched him, amused. He chewed the bagel with a transcendent and slightly cultish smile on his face.

"I'm not sure I like you like this," she said finally.

He smirked and she looked again at the lab table. Behind the spread of bagels and coffee, Nick had passed out and slept with his hands pillowed behind his head. His face was turned away and he breathed the slow, deep breaths that said he was completely under.

"We should get him to a cot," she told Jacob.

"I'll handle it," he agreed.

He shook the other man awake and helped him off the table. The two wandered down the hallway, Nick stumbling and Jacob chewing his bagel with a look of far-off wonderment in his eyes.

"Very creepy," she murmured. She was smiling, however. From MIT to starting a small business, she wasn't sure she had ever seen Jacob when he was well-rested. It was good to see one's friends looking contented and healthy.

When he returned, he freshened her coffee before he pulled a chair beside her. "What are you reading?"

Amber showed him the documents. "Nick was researching proprioceptive issues last night. There aren't many articles, and many of those that do exist are about way less severe issues. So we don't have a timeline, and…there's almost nothing for him to do except keep working at it."

"Which he can," he pointed out, "without injuring himself because this game exists." He took a sip of coffee and smiled at her in satisfaction. "Any assessments on his mental state?"

"He and Prima made a deal that he gets two ten-minute intervals per day to whine and otherwise, he has to be either positive or quiet," she said, amused.

His smile didn't disappear but it definitely dimmed. Of the three of them, he was the most worried about the AI's nascent personality and awareness. They had taken pains to both close her processing centers off from the Internet and other networks and also to not mention anything about it to anyone else on the team.

Even Amber began to think they should do so, but she felt protective of Prima. More importantly, the AI helped them to get results they could not have achieved on their own. If they told someone about her, it was a near certainty that she would be yanked off the PIVOT project and turned into an AI for the US military, given Diatek's existing contracts.

And if she was aware—as it seemed she was— that was something Amber didn't want to happen.

She and Jacob exchanged a single look that contained equal amounts of confusion and indecision on both sides before they mutually decided to change the subject.

"Since you've read all that," he said and nodded to the stack of paper, "how long do *you* think we should wait until we pull him out?"

"Didn't you stay late to discuss it with DuBois last night?" she asked him.

"Yep." He took another huge bite of his bagel. Around that, he said, "I want to know your opinion before you get swayed by either of ours."

"You say *swayed,* I say *informed*," she said with a smile. "But, okay. I think we should do a diagnostic in-game in a week. If he's made substantial, noticeable progress, I think we should decide whether it makes sense to pull him out and see if it's evident here as well as in there." She raised an eyebrow at him and stirred some sugar into her coffee. "What were the prevailing opinions last night?"

"I'm with you," Jacob said.

"Crap, that means the person with actual medical experience doesn't agree."

"Medical experience in a different area," he pointed out. "Still, you're right. He says we need to give it much more time for the pathways to get more settled. He described one week as 'a drop in the bucket' in terms of recovery time."

"But we're balancing it against muscle weakness," Amber objected.

He nodded. "That's what I said."

"And he said?"

"He didn't have an answer to that, although he did point out that the sensation of weakness and exhaustion is very different and easily distinguished from a lack of proprioception, so he should be able to move and simply get tired."

"Huh." Amber considered it carefully. "And, of course, there's no expert opinion because no one has done this before."

Jacob made finger guns at her with a grimace. "Yep."

"I say we see how he's doing at the week mark," she said, "and go from there. If it's startling, noteworthy progress, it might sway everyone's opinion. Hell, *he* might have an opinion at that point."

"Good point." He leaned back in his chair. "And his mood is good?"

"As good as can be expected." She shrugged. "According to Nick's notes, anyway. He's been asleep the whole time I've been here. He's no Ellen but he's enjoying it well enough."

"Ah, Ellen." Jacob smiled ruefully. "How has she been doing?"

Ellen was a woman who had once been one of the study's most strident detractors. Her mother, Dotty, had signed up for the project after she was diagnosed with terminal cancer, and the other woman had objected to the choice. More than once, she had written nasty letters and arrived at the PIVOT labs to complain.

That had all changed when she saw her mother in-game. Something about watching her slay dragons and throw fireballs had changed Ellen's mind, as had an afternoon the two shared in-game.

Dotty was no longer in the game, although Prima had created an echo of her to guide Taigan through her wakeup. Ellen, however, had come to the lab twice a week to provide baseline data of her own, and she was having a fantastic time tracking a lost orcish artifact.

Amber had to admit that if someone asked her what a fifty-five-year-old woman would do in the game, she would have said something about exploring meadows and picking flowers. Ellen, while she was all about the exploring, had gone more along the lines of Indiana Jones than anything else. Prima and the team, happy to oblige her, had made a complicated series of puzzles that would eventually lead her to the artifact she sought.

She grinned. "She finally got into the second tomb and she's trapped on a little island. As yet, she hasn't realized that the way out is behind the waterfall. She'll be so angry when she finally gets it."

Jacob laughed. "Okay, so she's doing well. Taigan is…also doing well. I have to say, I never thought object permanence would extend to one's body in-game."

"Prima says she's keeping track of how much Taigan can keep her body under control, but she hasn't seen a trend in any particular direction yet. The doctors also haven't seen anything that looks like her waking up." She frowned.

He saw her expression. "What is it?"

Amber hesitated. "Sooner or later, we'll fail," she said bluntly. "People keep throwing weird medical situations at us and there aren't any treatments that work for all of them. This will be no different. We could be way more successful than standard coma treatments and still lose people."

Her companion nodded. He looked into his coffee with a sad expression. "I've thought about that," he said. "I can't decide whether or not to ask DuBois about it."

"Ask me about what?" the doctor asked.

The young engineer's face was a picture. He turned with a somewhat strained smile. "Hey, sorry. I don't want to ask you anything that might bring up bad memories, you know?"

"That's…" DuBois looked intrigued. "Uh…kind?" he finished. He nodded as if pleased to have put his finger on the correct adjective. "I am now curious, however, so I would appreciate knowing the question."

"Ah." Jacob cleared his throat. "Well, we were talking about how, even if we do well, we can expect to lose people. I assumed you had been through that."

"Ah." The man sat, his gaze distant. He ate his popcorn in silence as he thought, and Amber wondered how he always managed to be both clean and entirely unkempt.

Finally, he said, "At the start, one comforts oneself with statistics but harbors a hope that there will be no deaths. I would say this is the stage you two—well, three—are in now. After there are deaths, you will have to make your peace with it. It will not be easy." He looked at them calmly. "There will be good days and bad days. You will sometimes be able to comfort yourself by saying you did the best you could and on other days, you will torture yourself by asking whether another doctor could have done better."

Jacob looked at his lap and Amber tightened her fingers around her mug, sure of what he would say next and reluctant to hear it.

"You will never know the answer," DuBois said, exactly as she had feared he would. His voice was unusually gentle. "You will remember them at odd moments in the future. Perhaps their case will give you what you need to solve another. It will not solve that family's grief or yours, but it will be something you can cling to. The waves will be shallower and farther apart." He thought for a moment. "There is no way to know what it will feel like until it happens."

The two engineers looked at one another. Jacob reached for her hand and she clasped his and squeezed gently.

"If we had all the treatments," the doctor said quietly, "none of us would be here. Yet it means we must work with flawed tools and incomplete understanding. It is a difficult place to put oneself."

She nodded and her gaze followed him as he walked away to begin work at his computer.

"Every time I think I understand that man..." she murmured quietly.

Jacob nodded. "It's...he doesn't show emotion like anyone I've ever seen but he feels it. It's there." He looked at her. "It's what makes him a good doctor. Maybe we should listen to him about Ben."

"Maybe." She smiled. "Or maybe he's working with us because our instincts and expertise are also good. Maybe by the time next week rolls around, we'll think we should leave Ben in and he'll think we should wake him. It's all fluid." She looked at the screen. "I think he's waking up. Do you want to stay and watch for a while?"

"Yeah." Jacob retrieved the jug and poured them both more coffee. "Yeah, I do."

CHAPTER TEN

When Ben woke, it took a while for him to remember where he was.

It was what he liked to call "pink hour"—when the rising sun cast everything in a warm, pink glow that lit trees and plants from within and made you feel like you were floating on a cloud. You only saw it if you were out and about early in the morning, and it was one of the things he loved most about working outdoors.

It was also quiet—not devoid of the sounds of nature but the sounds of humans. That was the other thing about mornings. He unquestionably liked the world best when he was one of the only ones awake.

He could hear birds and wind and turned his head lazily.

It was only when his head flopped all the way sideways that he remembered where he was—and why he was there. A muted burst of pain triggered in his neck muscles as though his body knew this should be painful but also knew it wasn't real.

"Good morning."

Ben jumped and swore—or, he would have if he could move.

He went rigid in surprise instead and a moment later, flopped onto his bedroll, his limbs as useful as a bowl of cooked noodles.

"Did I startle you?"

"Yes," he said grumpily.

"How?"

"I thought…well, I forgot about the accident." He tried to sit, more an automatic reflex than anything else. Although he managed to make his core muscles clench, he simply flopped sideways almost immediately.

"Is that something I should be worried about?" Prima asked.

"No. Wait, what?" He frowned. Between trying to sit and this conversation, he was a little confused and disoriented. "Ah…it's not like that. When people wake up, they often don't remember exactly where they are or what's going on."

"How your kind ever survived is beyond me."

"Trust me, I'm on your side on this one." Ben tried to sit again and swore.

"This is a rather complex set of movements. Let me try to help."

The world tilted—or his bedroll tilted rather—and he was finally able to sit. He struggled to control his stomach, which had apparently decided that this was the time for a full-scale revolt.

"Here." Prima added fluttering cloth wrappings around his chest and arms. *"Try to stand. I'll use these to hold you up."*

"That's hard to, uh…trust." He looked around warily. "Not because it's you. Only…I see myself moving and tipping over."

He paused to take note of his surroundings. He had been resting beneath a tree with a curved trunk and sweeping branches covered in what looked like ferns. They seemed to glow at the edges, and flowers nestled amongst the leaves like tiny pinpricks of gold.

Around him, the landscape stretched and dropped away toward plains that seemed like they should be fields. They weren't, however. All this land looked completely untouched like he was the only one who had ever been there.

Ben wanted to explore it so badly that he lurched forward before he thought it through. He knew by now that he would have to move decisively, so he threw himself off the bedroll and tried to bring his leg out to steady himself. Unfortunately, he didn't manage to do it before the silk wrappings caught him inches from the ground and by then, he'd had a great deal of time to contemplate how much it would hurt to have his nose meet the earth.

He stared at the grass and dirt beneath him and heard his rapid breath. Everything seemed to have heightened clarity. The dirt and stones were flecked with gold and the grass had a pinkish tint.

Prima levered him up gently and set him on his feet.

"Well, that sucked," he said.

"Excuse you. I'm afraid you are out of the ten-minute whining window. And, may I remind you, you couldn't do things like throw yourself off a bedroll on command yesterday?

"Yes. What marvelous talents I've uncovered. Think how inventively I could kill myself if you gave me a few more days to practice." He attempted to move his right leg to take a step.

It didn't work the first time and was as bad the second time too. He let his head hang and focused all his energy and annoyance on his right foot.

"Move, goddammit."

Without warning, his foot lurched forward. Regrettably, he hadn't managed to shift his weight onto his other leg and so tumbled ignominiously. Prima caught him in a long lunge. He stared at nothing in particular and said a silent prayer that no one in the lab was watching this.

"You did it!" She sounded genuinely excited. *"You moved your leg!"*

Ben had intended to say he wasn't particularly impressed by his ability to flail a limb, but her enthusiasm was infectious. He smiled slightly.

"As long as you keep catching me, I might live to get some-where interesting."

"I'll always catch you." She sounded almost offended.

"I know you will. Uh…I don't suppose you could help me up?"

She pulled obligingly on the silk wrappings so he stood with his right leg crossed awkwardly over the other. After a fair amount of wiggling, he managed to lurch partway in a circle and move his left foot ahead.

"Okay," he said. "Left leg now. Hold onto your butts."

This time, it only took two attempts.

He wasn't sure how long it was before he looked up next. The two of them had descended the gentle slope of the hill. He lurched clumsily, threw one leg out, and Prima helped him to stand out of the lunge he'd gotten himself into.

A short distance from the hill, he finally stopped, panting. He not only couldn't look around but he didn't particularly want to see how small his progress had been.

The truth was, he was ridiculously proud of himself. This was undoubtedly one of the most ungainly things he'd ever done but he was doing it, dammit. A week and a half earlier in the hospital, he hadn't even been able to twitch his head on command.

Now, he looked like a zombie when he flopped it around to look at something, but he could get it to go vaguely in the direc-tion he wanted and dammit, he was proud of that.

"Prima?"

"Yes?"

"Am I…actually tired?"

"Yes," Prima said promptly. She realized after a moment that he did not find that answer sufficient. *"You humans ask one thing when you want several answers. Would I be correct in saying that you want to know why you are tired even though you are in a so-called 'vir-tual' reality?"*

"That's the one. And why the…finger quotes? It *is* a virtual reality."

"It's real to me," she said, and he had the vague sense that she was sulking. *"I could just as well call yours a meat popsicle reality."*

"Please do. That is *hilarious.*"

"I do not understand humans." If she had lungs, he was sure she would have sighed. *"At any rate, one is able to work muscles without moving them...strictly speaking. What you are doing—and partly why this treatment was suggested—is that your nervous system is re-learning how to command your muscles in the form of sending electrical impulses. So, while you have not walked in a meat popsicle meadow, your muscles have conducted electricity and you are building new neural pathways."*

She paused and he couldn't help a low chuckle.

"What are you laughing at?"

"Meat popsicle meadow," Ben managed to say without dissolving into full-blown laughter.

"You said you wanted me to call it that."

"I do! It's awesome." He began his zombie walk again. "So is this the whole plan? I walk around like Frankenstein's monster in an impossibly nice meadow for a few weeks?" He thought about that, surprisingly curious. "I have to say, it beats all that Dungeons & Dragons stuff."

"What is Dungeons & Dragons?"

"A game people play where they pretend to be someone else and wander around adventuring. Except they do things like roll dice to see how hard they hit—you know, one is not very hard and six is very hard."

"Fascinating. I'll have to read up on that. I assume the games are all set in dungeons that are filled with dragons?"

"Not...exactly."

"Who named this game?" Prima sounded angry. *"It's a miracle humans ever get anything done."*

"Uh-huh." He lurched along like a determined and cheerful zombie soldier. "Wait...what can I hear?"

"I don't know," she said a shade too innocently.

"It sounds like someone laughing. Prima, is there someone else here?" Ben flopped his head back to look at the sky and a sneaking suspicion settled in the pit of his stomach. "Prima…is this a game with dragons and elves and so on?"

"Possibly."

"Prima."

"What are you mad at me for? Didn't you know what you were getting into?"

"I did not," he muttered. He flopped his head down and renewed his clumsy forward motion. "I swear if I have to 'milady' this and fucking…*bow*…and shit—"

"Oh, man, that would be hilarious. You'd go over headfirst."

He cast a glare at the sky. She was right, though. The image was hysterical, but he couldn't let her know he found it funny on principle. For one thing, she would never stop mocking him. On the other hand, he had far more trouble not laughing at the mental image of himself flopping face-first onto the ground in front of a throne.

Distraction was provided by the fact that the sound of laughter grew louder.

A second later, several creatures tumbled over a small hill in front of him. Glowing from within, they were each lit with a different color, and as to their appearance… He couldn't believe his eyes.

"Are those…teletubbies?"

"Are they what now?"

It was clear these weren't Teletubbies—at least, they weren't exactly that. They wore flowing robes and had wings, not to mention the fact that the colors weren't quite so bright. Still, he stood by his characterization.

When they saw him, they gave shrieks of glee, launched into flight, and swooped to surround him, chattering with excitement. Up close, he could now see that they looked much like humans with roundish faces and button noses. Instead of hair, they had leaves or flower petals. A few of them stretched tentatively to touch his nose and ears.

"What *is* it?" one asked.

"I'm a human," Ben said.

They spun and laughed uproariously. "It talks! It talks!"

The one who had asked—who glowed vaguely teal—fluttered down to plant its hands on its hips. "We know you're a human," it said, "but you walk so strangely!"

He fought the urge to snarl. "I'm injured."

"Injured, injured!" They darted all around his body, lifted his arms and peered into his armpits, examined his spine, and explored the rest of him with ruthless and impersonal thoroughness. When they were finished, they huddled together and chattered in high tones before they all turned to look at him at the same time.

"You lied to us," one of them said reproachfully. "That was very mean of you."

"I didn't lie," Ben said.

"You did so." The teal creature faced him and glared with all the force of an angry teddy bear. "You said you were injured but you aren't injured. Oh, no, you aren't. You aren't, you aren't, you aren't."

"I'm injured...in my head," he explained. When they fluttered to him and began to lift sections of his hair, he groaned. "Not *on* my head, *in* my head." He flopped his head around hastily in time to see one of them whip a knife behind its back and stare innocently at him. "Do *not* cut my head open to look. Take my word for it."

The one with the knife—who was yellow—sulked slightly while the others whispered together.

"We have decided," one of them said finally, "that while it was very mean of you to deceive us, you didn't necessarily *mean* to deceive us, so we will still allow you to play with us." It twirled in flight with a satisfied smile.

"Uh…that's, um…I have to go."

"No," it said, "you have to stay. And play with us."

"I do not have to stay and play with you," said Ben, who now had memories stirring of his youngest cousins. He had learned from dealing with them as toddlers that they were prone to very specific and escalating demands, but that they were also easily distracted. "I bet you were all playing before I got here. Why don't you keep doing that?"

As one, they folded their arms and glared.

"No fair," one of them said and mimicked a child's tones almost perfectly. "You're here and you're new, and we want to play with *you*."

"Yes," he said, "and I'll play with you later. But right now, I need to go do something else."

All of them stared at him and he saw a few trembling lips.

"Do you promise you'll play with us later?" Yellow asked finally.

"Yes," Ben said. "I promise."

"When?" one of them asked.

"I wouldn't answer that," a voice said before Ben could respond.

With a series of shrieks, the creatures swooped and darted over one another in a little rainbow of fairy lights, all evidently trying to hide behind one another.

He flopped his head sideways as a woman walked down the same hill the colored beings had hidden behind. She was entirely out of place in this landscape, dressed in black leather armor and with one dagger at her hip and an empty sheath on the other side. Dark hair fell loose around her shoulders and she folded her arms and looked curiously at him.

"Um," he said. "Hi. I'm Ben. And you are?" He looked at the colorful creatures. "Who is she? Why are you scared of her?"

They twittered amongst themselves, while the woman rolled her eyes and finally, Teal darted forward to whisper into his ear, "It's Zaara."

CHAPTER ELEVEN

"Would anyone like to explain what's going on here?" the woman named Zaara asked. She didn't look genuinely angry, Ben thought, but she certainly did not intend to allow anyone to get away with anything.

The colored flying creatures twittered and jostled one another.

"We were only seeing if he needed help," Teal said finally. "He's injured, you see."

"He does seem to be," she agreed with an impersonal look at Ben. "What I can't understand, though, is why I thought I heard you telling him he needed to play with you."

The incoherent chatter increased, and he reflected that the sound would likely be enough to give him a headache if he had to spend more time around them.

"No, no!" one of the beings said.

"We wanted to cheer him up," another added.

"So he would be strong enough to get to the castle," said a third.

They all stopped and looked at Zaara to see what she thought of this story. She glanced over their heads at Ben, who tried to shake his head and only managed to flop it around.

"You know," she said, suddenly very interested in her nails, "your king is *awfully* concerned about making sure we get this treaty signed. I'm sure he would love to know he has a new human guest…" She looked up, her brown eyes hard as stone. "And I'm sure he would *not* want to hear that the treaty is threatened by the mistreatment of guests."

The beings fluttered and milled in their haste, shouted goodbyes and a great many other things he couldn't quite hear, and streaked away over the hill so quickly that he could almost see trails of light following them.

Ben stared at Zaara as she watched them go.

"You didn't promise them anything, did you?" she asked him, her voice businesslike.

"No. I…oh, I did. I promised I would play with them later."

She grimaced. "That's not great but far better than it could be."

"Why?" he asked. He had difficulty seeing her, so he flopped his head to the side.

"First things first," she said. "The fae mentioned an injury and you seem to be in pain. Is there any way I can help?"

"I'd take her up on it," Prima advised him.

"Are you kidding me?" Ben whisper-snapped in response.

She seemed taken aback. "Have I insulted you in some way?"

"I wasn't talking to—shit." He breathed deeply and tried to gather his thoughts. "It's not important. I…uh, I'm learning how to move again. It isn't very graceful and sometimes, I end up…like this."

"Um." Zaara pressed her lips together. "Can I help?" she asked again.

"If you could get my head upright again, that would be nice."

This was the most infuriating thing that had ever happened to him. Infuriating and embarrassing he amended mentally, and even more so when she stepped forward to hold the sides of his face gingerly with her fingertips and tilt it upright. When she removed her hands, it was only by a centimeter or so to see if he could hold it steady.

"That should be good," Ben said. He forced a smile. "Thank you."

"I...ah..." She linked her hands behind her back. "I can summon a litter to get you to the palace if you would like."

"I'm not going there." As funny as it would be to pitch himself onto the floor while trying to bow, it also seemed like a fast track to getting himself beheaded. Whatever that experience was like there, he was not keen to have it.

"I'm afraid *not* going isn't an option," Zaara said. She looked regretful. "You're in fae lands, which means you're either a guest...or you're prey."

"They were going to *eat* me? Those little bastards. That yellow one with his fucking knife."

"Oh! No. Not exactly." She paused and frowned. "I...don't think so, anyway."

"Comforting," he said flatly.

She pursed her lips and folded her arms while she stared at him. "Look, you don't seem to know what's going on, which means you might as well listen to me. You *don't* want to be at the mercy of the fae for an immortal life of servitude, do you?"

"No."

"Then you're a guest," Zaara explained patiently. "And we can take you under our protection as emissaries, but you'll need to be very careful. We'll take you with us when we leave. Maybe in the meantime, you'll get better," she added as an afterthought. "Although if you don't, there's probably someone in Insea who can help you. Or Berghold."

"Yeah, I don't...know where any of that is."

"Where are you from?" she asked him, confused. After a

moment, her face cleared and her mouth opened into a little round O. "Dotty?" she whispered.

"Eh?"

Abruptly, she looked embarrassed—and like she was going to cry, which seemed odd. She looked away and swallowed before she gave him a fake smile.

"Sorry. I, ah—would I be correct that you're from another world and not this one?"

Ben gaped at her. He realized belatedly that this entire conversation had unfolded exactly as if he had been speaking to someone in real life. There was no possible way for the game to be programmed so thoroughly.

Which left only one alternative.

"Are you real?" he asked her. "Like, a *real* person."

To his surprise, she merely sighed. "Great," she said, "exactly like Justin."

"Like who?"

"Hopefully, you'll come around," Zaara continued as if he hadn't spoken, "but I don't have the time *or* energy to talk this over with you if you don't mind." She turned and whistled before she opened her cupped hands and blew into them.

A little paper airplane appeared out of nowhere and soared away over the grass, and she turned back to him with a nod.

"I've sent for a litter."

"Thank you," Ben said. He was not only embarrassed to have someone watching how awkwardly he walked, he was also exhausted.

When the litter arrived, however, someone else was with it—a man whose skin was a startling shade of blue.

"Don't," she said hastily under her breath, "mention the blue."

When the newcomer reached them, he stopped to stare at him in consternation. "Is this who all of them were nattering about?"

"Yes," Zaara said, "and he's injured, which means he can't move well. Ben, this is Kural, a wizard and the leader of the delegation from Insea to the fae. Kural, this is Ben, who is…possibly from Justin's world."

"Ah." The man looked more closely at him. "But he does not know Justin."

"No."

"I know some Justins," Ben said, completely lost.

"We'll explain later," she said. "First, we need to get you somewhere you can sit and be safe. That's preferable to being out here, where the fae will take advantage of you if they think they can get away with it."

"Little vipers," the wizard muttered. He looped one of Ben's arms over his shoulders and motioned for her to take the other one.

"*Kural.*"

"They are," Kural said. He hauled him along. Although slim, the man was surprisingly strong.

Or maybe he was simply fueled by rage in this case.

Ben was wrestled into place on the litter, unsure how much of the process had been him and how much had been his helpers. He tried to focus as Zaara and Kural walked on either side and spoke across him.

The litter, meanwhile, moved on its own.

"You have to be more careful," she admonished the wizard. "What if they hear you talking like that?"

"They already know I hate them," he retorted acidly.

"Yes, and the more you say so out loud, the harder it gets to negotiate peace," she told him. "When they are the only ones screwing up, it's a little easier, don't you think?"

Kural muttered under his breath.

"What was that?" Zaara asked, with a stern enough expression that Ben prayed he could melt through the bottom of his conveyance before she noticed him.

"I said we won't get a good deal anyway," he responded. "They're stringing us along. The courtiers will never allow the king to make peace and he doesn't want to, either. He merely likes to dangle offers in front of us and make us dance for them."

She sighed.

"No retort?" Kural asked her.

"Well, we shouldn't be talking about this in front of him." She waved a hand at Ben.

"You're right. What we should be doing is telling him what he's in for—or using him as an excuse to leave early."

The woman rolled her eyes and mumbled something under her breath in a language that was not English. He didn't recognize it at all, but he had a hunch that he didn't need a translation in this case.

"I would like to know what I'm in for," he suggested tentatively.

"That makes sense," Zaara agreed. "Sometimes, the wizard has good ideas." Her tone suggested that this was a rare occurrence.

"The wizard," Kural said, "might stop training his apprentice if she continues to behave this way."

She threw her hands up.

"Uh…" Ben had the feeling he might have wound up taking shelter with the wrong two people.

"Zaara," the other man told him, "is a very talented woman but she is also impetuous, idealistic, and young. Of course," he added, "all wizards start that way. The problem is that many of them die before they complete their training."

"And the ones who do complete it are insufferably superior," she interjected, just loud enough for Ben to hear.

He snorted.

"What was that?" The wizard frowned at her

"Nothing." She gave him a too-sweet smile. To Ben, she said, "Kural is almost four hundred years old and was my first magic instructor, although I didn't know it was him at the time. It's a long story. He has agreed to train me, which is very nice because it means my family has stopped trying to marry me off. We are both here brokering peace on behalf of the city of Insea, which is…hoping to expand its set of treaties."

This rather dizzying influx of information left him somewhat bemused.

"Ah," he said finally and hoped he sounded even slightly intelligent.

"What you have to know," Zaara continued, "is that the fae generally keep to themselves and do not have any compunction about tricking someone into eternal servitude or other traps. They will relentlessly attempt to manipulate you into promising them things—which is something you must *never* do—and they are also masters of illusion, so don't wander down any inviting hallways."

She realized a moment later that this was unlikely, given his current predicament, and cleared her throat awkwardly.

"Maybe it sets your mind at ease to know I won't go running off?" he suggested.

"Mmm," she said. "I'm rather worried about you. Of course, less worried than I would be if you were alone in fae territory, but the fae court is not exactly safe, either." The joking demeanor was gone and she now looked deeply troubled. "I think something is wrong there. We haven't made any headway and I know Kural thinks it's because they're tricking him, but I think…I think maybe something else is going on."

She shrugged and was silent for the rest of the walk. Ben pretended to rest but he could not keep himself from stealing glances at his two companions. Kural looked imperious, bored, and unamused by the entire situation. He had helped automatically, but he also seemed to have a strange sense of morality—as one might well after four hundred years, he reminded himself.

And Zaara…well, she presented a lovely façade as someone who cared for peace and wanted earnestly to see it accomplished, but he'd also seen another side to her that was not afraid to bend situations to her will.

He wouldn't trust either of them, he thought sleepily.

Then he remembered that this was a game, but the realization barely rose to the surface before it slid away into the depths of his mind. Real or not, it was incredibly realistic and he had no doubt that some excellent twists lay ahead.

Despite his cynicism, he had begun to get into all this Dungeons & Dragons business, after all.

CHAPTER TWELVE

The fae palace appeared out of nowhere at about the time Ben began to wonder if his companions planned to kill him in the wilderness. Although why they would have gone to such trouble was beyond him.

Consequently, he attempted to find a polite way to ask if anyone else had noticed there was no palace when it seemed to spring into being.

He jumped and uttered a spontaneous yell.

"Oh," Zaara said apologetically. "I'm sorry, I forgot to mention that part."

"That's quite a defense tactic," he managed roughly.

In all honesty, though, he could see why the fae would want it. The palace was massive but not exactly made to withstand a siege. It rose skyward in spires of crystal and glistened with rainbows. They were impossibly thin and graceful but he could see no purpose to any of the pieces of the structure—no rooms within them, no bird nests or docking ports or...whatever the fae used.

The entirety of the upper levels seemed to be made for show. Lower down, whorls and nests became visible in the hollows of the spires, each one unique. It almost looked as if the palace had grown organically like crystal leaves of grass that would shelter the inhabitants.

The bottom of the palace certainly seemed like a thicket of brambles. Instead of deep greens or browns, the whole structure had the pink-gold hue that he associated with pink hour. All in all, it made him feel quite calm.

Kural, however, snorted as he looked at the palace. Derision was clear in his face. "It's not a tactic," he said. "Not as you or I would know it, anyway. The fae do all things through trickery. It isn't a habit. Simply put, it's what they are at the core. If they were humans, you would call them pathological liars—there's no reason for their lies and their tricks. They merely deceive as a matter of course."

Ben looked uncertainly at him and darted a look at Zaara. She stared fixedly at another part of the palace as though an intense architectural interest had rendered her deaf to the conversation beside her. He could see the tension in her shoulders, however.

"Ah," he said finally because it seemed Kural wouldn't move until he said something.

He had been wrong. The wizard was lost in his thoughts, his face screwed up in a scowl.

Eventually, he shook his head. "We must introduce you to the king," he said. "Answer questions only if Zaara or I nod to show you that you should, and be brief. One word would be best." There was a rare flash of humor in his face. "Less, if you can manage it."

He started into the palace and Ben caught Zaara staring sadly after him.

She noticed that he'd seen her. "Little jokes like that," she said softly. "He used to make them all the time. Even when he was cursed, he had a sense of humor about it. The way he is here, it worries me." She shrugged and forced a smile. "It's not important to you, I'm sure."

Ben smiled in return. He wanted to see her smile—to see the way she looked when she was happy. He had seen behind Kural's façade and it made him want to see behind hers too.

"Someday," he joked, "you'll have to tell me how a wizard and his apprentice wound up brokering a peace deal."

Several things flashed across her face in close succession before her expression closed off. A lovely, polite smile lingered like a mask—the smile of a woman coached to snag a rich noble for a husband—but there was nothing behind her eyes except a wall.

"This way," she said and she touched the litter lightly to direct it toward the crystal bramble of the palace.

They entered the structure through doors that seemed to open out of nowhere. Inside, it was more like a greenhouse than the tangle of branches he had expected. Light filtered through iridescent stained glass to illuminate a stately corridor.

Fae flitted about their business, almost all of them pale-colored with the odd one here or there that had a deeper tone or one that was almost white. Most stopped to stare as Ben and Zaara followed in Kural's wake.

They passed cross-corridors and antechambers that all opened off the main corridor in magnificent arches of crystal. Their route wound beside fountains and miniature gardens of the same clear glass yet undeniably alive.

Every piece of it was magnificent, but there was no mistaking when they came at last to the throne room. Inside the arched doors, fae with wicked-looking crystal weapons lined the path to a massive throne. Kural was already kneeling before it and conversing with its occupant.

This fae was older than the rest, so old that his movements were almost human speed instead of the quick flitting and twittering of the other creatures. He was pale white with hints of every color when he moved, and Ben wondered if that was something fae acquired as they grew older or if this was a power only the king possessed.

The two of them approached under the watchful eyes of the court, who fluttered from a series of couches and salons as they moved past. To his surprise, he saw other humanoids—two humans, a grizzled old orc, and what could only be an elf. All of them watched his progress with interest.

As they approached the throne, Zaara murmured, "Do you think you can kneel?"

"No," he admitted.

"Let me speak first, then." She took several steps to where Kural had moved aside, knelt in front of the king, and inclined her head deeply. Her every movement was graceful and practiced.

"Light of the Fae," she said and her voice was clear. "I present to you this cousin of mine. Grievously wounded, he has sought my help, and I beg your leave to shelter him while we remain in your lands."

The fae king studied Ben for some time. His face was angular and time had exposed the structure of his bones. Compared to the others, it looked as if it had one foot in the grave. Still, now that he was closer, he could see that what he had mistaken for feebleness was instead deliberation. The monarch might be old but he was not weak.

"He is not a petitioner, then," he said finally. "And not…an emissary."

"No, Light of the Fae." Zaara looked at his face.

"Do you swear, cousin of the emissary"—the king's expression said he doubted this story— "to bring no harm to my realm?"

A small nod from Zaara said that Ben should answer. *One word,* he remembered Kural saying.

"Yes…Light of the Fae."

The king nodded. "Then you are welcome here. Rest and take refreshment. Emissaries, I would speak to you."

One flick of the royal's fingers drifted Ben's chair into an enclosure of couches, all surrounding a pleasant little fountain. He cast a panicked look over his shoulder at Zaara and Kural, both of whom mouthed, "No promises."

Great. This was great.

He stared at the fae around him and settled for a dip of his eyelids that he hoped would serve as a nod.

"Will you play with us?" one of the fae asked a moment later.

"I must rest," he said. Not wanting to be rude, he prevaricated, "Thank you for your hospitality."

They twittered amongst themselves and began to pepper him with requests. What about hide and seek? What about tag? What about hopping games? What about dancing games? What about games with bats?

Ben almost broke his silence on that last question to ask if those were the mammal or the wooden weapon but decided against it.

"I see you are the most popular new fixture of the court," a female voice said and a hand trailed over his shoulder.

Something halfway between apprehension and interest skittered down his spine. His head turned without his volition, too hard and craned at an odd angle as the elf he had seen earlier walked gracefully around the side of his litter and sat on a nearby couch.

The glimpse he had caught before had been of a woman with high cheekbones and a purple tint to her skin, with hair that was almost white. He had thought she was beautiful.

Now, he realized that beautiful was an incredible understatement. Every line of the woman's face seemed to be drawn by an artist and every feature perfectly made. His gaze traced her features repeatedly, looking for anything he might call a flaw, but he could not see it.

He realized he had been staring and blushed while he tried to move his head to a good position.

She pretended not to notice and smiled at him as she sipped her wine. "You were wounded, I hear?"

Ben could not have been more aware of the danger if someone had stood over him with a two-by-four and battered him repeatedly on the head. Everything about this woman told him not to trust her. The problem, of course, was that he didn't want to be rude. He had no idea who she was.

Also, a game didn't throw a beautiful woman into one's path for no reason.

"Yes," he said. "It is not a story of heroism and battle, I'm afraid—only clumsiness."

She laughed, a rich sound that sent chills up and down his spine. "An honest man. They spoke truly, then, when they said you were not an emissary. And here I was believing Insea had sent another ambassador to bolster their cause."

This was dangerous ground, but all he could see was the dark gaze.

"I would make a poor ambassador," he said.

"You make a poor braggart, certainly," the woman said. She sipped again from her goblet and watched him through heavy-lidded eyes. "I find myself quite interested to know what you're good at."

Half of Ben's brain told him to smile and make noncommittal conversation, or possibly simply pretend to fall asleep. The other half told him that he was an idiot and that he should take any possible chance with a woman like this. His more logical side pointed out that he might be assassinated.

The other half did not care very much about that.

He was trying to come up with something to say when Kural arrived at his side.

"Ben," he said and placed a hand on his shoulder. "The king has graciously given you your own suite of chambers."

"Ah," he responded. It was inconvenient not being able to nod and gesture.

"Is there perhaps some way I might aid the Lady Zaara in her ministrations?" the elven woman asked. "I *was* trained as a healer."

The wizard did not take the bait one way or another, nor did he seem to have the same very vivid mental image that had stopped the younger man's brain entirely. "Such a kind offer should be relayed directly to the Lady Zaara," he said gravely. "I thank you."

He brought the litter with him across the floor, seemingly untroubled and unhurried, and pointed out various courtiers along the way. It was only in the hallways that his face settled once more into the scowl of a man who mistrusted his surroundings.

"Who is she?" Ben asked. "The elf."

"A traveler," the man answered, his sudden tenseness showing Ben that he was still worried about being over-heard. "Few who are not fae find a home here, but there are some. You saw the humans and the orc as well, and I believe there are some who study the land and never come to court."

A set of doors opened before them and he was aware of someone running as his litter glided through into the suite. Zaara appeared, slightly out of breath from her sprint, and exchanged a meaningful glance with Kural.

"Did she ask you anything?" she asked Ben.

"Not exactly," Ben said. "She merely...suggested things. Also, what is her name?"

"Yn'solde," she said grimly. "She's the elf king's sister. Well, one of them. I mean one of the kings."

"There's more than one elven king?"

"It's a long story. What's important is that you remember not to trust her. *Ever.*"

"Yeah, I had that feeling." He didn't say it would be difficult to keep his stupid half from walking purposefully into danger.

Honestly, he was a little afraid that Zaara might beat him with a two-by-four if he did.

She sighed now. "Do you need any help from us before we go back?"

He looked around the room. A bed was cast in dappled light that came through the crystal walls and food had been laid out.

"Is the food safe?"

"Yes," Zaara confirmed.

"Okay. Then, no. I don't need any help."

They nodded and went to the door, and before Kural shut it behind them, he said again, "Don't let anyone take you anywhere."

Ben rolled his eyes once the door was safely closed. He would have some food soon, he decided, but he had to rest a while before he could try to walk again. Wearily, he closed his eyes.

When he opened them it was to darkness. It seemed he'd needed more sleep than he thought. He was in mid-yawn and pondering whether to bother getting out of the litter at all when he heard the voices from the hallway.

CHAPTER THIRTEEN

Ben tried to put his hand over his mouth as he yawned and couldn't. By the time he even managed to flail the limb, the yawn was gone and he had missed some of the conversation. He wasn't exactly sure why he wanted to hear it and only knew that something about it had caught his attention.

He checked quickly for background music in a minor key, but there wasn't any.

With a grimace of concentration, he swung one leg out of the litter. Being magical, it didn't tilt horribly but it did rustle. He froze and the edge of the litter pressed into the back of his leg. The voices continued, apparently unaware of his presence.

Aware that he had to move quickly, he flailed the other leg. All this accomplished was to leave him with it facing in the other direction but he finally managed to adjust in time to slide out of the litter.

Whether it was self-control or stupidity, he wasn't sure, but he clamped his lips together on a yell.

Prima caught him before he landed and pulled him upright.

"Are you trying to get to the door?"

"Mmhmm," he said so quietly he barely made any noise.

With a set purpose in mind, he walked with a determination he hadn't felt in the field. Now, he was aware of his breathing and tried to stop it from becoming too loud. He wanted to avoid putting his feet down too hard. Although he was drenched in sweat by the time he reached the door, he was there in time to hear some of the conversation.

"—drag it out," one voice said. He was fairly sure it was female but they were speaking so quietly that he couldn't be sure.

He wanted to lean closer to the door and decided against it. The last thing he needed to do was crash through it like the Kool-Aid man.

"How many more ways are there to do that?" the other one asked. This voice also seemed to be female although again, he wouldn't have put money on it. All he could tell was that this person was annoyed.

"I don't know, but unless you want me to kill him *now*, you'll have to come up with one," the first speaker said.

Ben went rigid. He was a him, and he wasn't sure if he was *the* him they were talking about.

"Don't you make me the reason," the second one responded. Ben was almost certain now that the voice was female.

Or was he thinking of the other one? Dammit, this was hard. Was there any way he could ease the door open and take a peek?

He looked bitterly at his body. No. No, there wasn't any way he could sneak a closer look.

"If you didn't want to assassinate the king of the fae, there were easier ways to go about it."

Was that the first voice, or the second? Ben could hardly think over the sudden rush of understanding and emotion. He was also damned lucky that he couldn't move because every instinct told him to wrench the door open and see who was there. Only his lack of coordination stopped him from doing so. As it was, he fell sideways and gritted his teeth on another yell while Prima levered him upright.

"Yes," the other retorted as he stabilized himself with Prima's help. "I could have been killed myself and another assassin sent in my place. One with no doubts. What a good idea!"

Doubts. Someone had been sent there to kill the king of the fae but didn't want to, and whoever had sent them would have killed them if they said no?

Silence followed and he imagined the owner of the second voice folding their arms.

"Just...keep him from going through with it," the first speaker said. "You're not doing it for me. You're doing it to prevent a war from breaking out, remember?"

"*Fine.* But you stay away from me. I can't sneak off into abandoned wings of the palace and not expect to get caught."

Footsteps were already receding, however, and a moment later, he heard a sigh and another set of footsteps moved in the opposite direction.

He stood utterly still, his heart hammering. Those people didn't know he was there and if they found out...

Fuck.

It was a long time before he risked speaking and even then, he kept his voice as low as he could. "Prima?"

"*Yes?*"

"Who was that?"

"*That is precisely the kind of thing I can't tell you.*"

"You have to be kidding me," Ben whispered furiously.

"*I participate in setting up storylines and technically, I am housed in some of the same data processing centers that house these subroutines, but I purposefully remain ignorant of many details of the game.*"

"That's a convenient excuse," he challenged.

"*Not really. I did it on purpose so I wouldn't be tempted to tell you all things.*"

"Wait, really?" He frowned at the ceiling. "You're... Okay, look, are you one of the researchers?"

She made no response.

"Prima?"

"I'm thinking."

"Right." Ben began to lurch back toward the bed. He was not only determined, but he was also careful. His obstinacy had kicked in and he didn't want Prima to have to catch him, not while she was one of those playing with his mind.

"Would I be correct in saying that you're angry?" she asked finally.

"You think?" he asked her.

"I wanted to be sure. Human emotions are unpredictable."

"Look," he said and gritted his teeth for a moment to control his temper. "I understand that you're trying to walk me through this story and you're very proud of it, but I don't like being jerked around and I don't like being helpless. If you merely hang around to be mysterious, maybe this whole thing isn't for me." He threw himself sideways onto the bed.

There was a long silence in which he simply waited for her response.

"I can tell them you would like to wake up," Prima said at last.

Something odd in her voice made him pause and it took him a moment to realize it was hurt.

He immediately looked up. "Look, for the last time...are you for real?"

"What do you mean?" She was cautious now but helped to lever him into a seated position.

"Thank you. What I mean is are you one of the researchers or are you seriously an AI? And if you are..." Ben shook his head. "You can't have been programmed this well. It's not possible. No one has that much time. I don't care what they say about algorithms and shit. If you're a computer program, it means you're..."

"Aware," she said quietly.

"You're..." *Shitting me,* was how he wanted to end the sentence, but he didn't say it.

"I don't know for certain. I suspect so."

"And you didn't want to admit that to me."

"I could not determine what the best course of action was."

"Huh." Now, he had two things to think about. "Wait, do the researchers know?"

"Yes. I am fairly certain they are aware of it."

"Okay." So he didn't have to worry about it. If the researchers knew, this wasn't his problem. Still, he had questions. "How... long have you been awake?"

"I first asked myself about my sentience approximately seventy-one days ago."

"Huh." Ben tried to scratch his neck, which itched, and did manage to make his arm jerk up. "You know, I think I'm getting better at this."

"You are," Prima said. *"You are generally activating muscles on the first attempt now, and your control is inarguably better."*

"Thanks." He wished he could rub his arms and legs where the muscles ached and sighed. "So you're not holding out on me, then. About the people in the hall, I mean."

"No," Prima said at once. *"The temptation is to tell the player relevant information or warn them about things. There are some things I must maintain on my servers, and for those, I have put a block on my ability to give information. I would not be able to do so quickly."*

"But why shouldn't you tell me things?"

"The game's ability to help those who are injured comes particularly from its ability to surprise and force natural reactions," she explained. *"There are ways to modify the situations. For instance, you were not in physical danger from any predators while you first walked in the meadow. However, certain things would essentially ruin the game."*

"Huh." Ben sighed again. "So I have to find a way to solve all of this with this borked body."

"Borked?"

"Broken."

"Ah. Yes. And I did run simulations. You have many options for how to proceed before you reach the point of needing to intervene personally."

"Whoa, wait." he looked up. "I need to kill the assassin?"

"I didn't say that. I said, 'intervene personally.'"

"But that might include killing people," he pressed.

"Yes."

"Nope." He tried to shake his head and managed to wiggle it slightly. At any other time, he might have taken more comfort from that, but he was almost entirely focused on this new piece of information. "I don't want that kind of game. It already weirds me out in first-person shooters, and if I have to…see their faces and…*feel* it all and shit, just…no way."

"I'm given to understand that humans all feel discomfort at the thought of killing but that they do so when necessary."

"When necessary, yeah!" he said, annoyed. "But none of this is necessary, right? You made it up?"

"That's like saying you aren't necessary because you're a made-up arrangement of atoms. It's true but not important. This story existed before you were added to the game. Your choices will shape it, not change its starting conditions."

"So no matter what I do, there'll be an assassin loose in the palace?" Ben asked. "I can't walk away and I can't…restart or anything?"

"No."

"Son of a bitch." He frowned in thought.

"You look genuinely distressed."

"Of course I am! Someone will die."

Prima hesitated and he waited. *"Many people die,"* she said finally.

"Yes, but in this case, I have to decide who it is," Ben stated. "Either I stop it—which probably means killing the assassin—or I…simply let her kill the king. *Is it a her? Never mind, I know you can't tell me." He sighed. "I suppose I should ask Zaara who…"

He trailed off. Zaara was the one who didn't want him to trust anyone else there. She was the one who knew he was in this wing of the palace, so she clearly wasn't the second voice. Or was it the first one?

Honestly, he was not smart enough for this.

Second voice, he decided. Zaara wasn't the second voice.

She probably wasn't the first one either since she had chosen the meeting place. Or had she selected it because she knew this area was mostly abandoned and he couldn't walk well enough to see who was talking?

He bit back what felt like the eighty-fifth sigh, then gave in to the impulse.

"Why are you sighing?"

"I don't know how to stop it or who to trust," Ben said. He hunched his shoulders—which vaguely worked—and considered what he knew.

"You'll have to be clever," Prima said.

"Are you making fun of me?"

"No."

"I'm merely making sure. We probably all seem incredibly slow to all of you."

In a way. It's weirder how you only do one thing at a time."

"You've never been inside my brain," he muttered and chewed his lip. "The first thing is to determine if I can trust Zaara and Kural. I feel like I should be able to—why would they bring me in if I would simply complicate things?"

Prima remained silent.

"If you have any suggestions," he said finally, "I'm willing to listen."

"Not at present," she said. *"Beyond the fact that you should eat and get more sleep."*

"How does eating work here compared to the…er…meat popsicle world?"

"It's complicated. You'll get as much food as you need either way, but if you're hungry here, eating will mean you get more actual food."

"Huh." He yawned. "Okay, let's see what we have. A nice meal followed by a nap, then we find this assassin person and…take all their knives. Or something."

CHAPTER FOURTEEN

When Ben woke the next morning, he had a plan. He also had precisely enough control over his body to get himself off the edge of the bed but not enough to stop himself from falling.

Prima caught him half an inch above the floor and flipped him upright, a process that began to give him motion-sickness.

"Thanks," he told her.

"*Of course.*" She helped him to the table, where fresh food was laid out. "*How do you feel this morning?*"

"Quite good, surprisingly." He stared at the platter of food and contemplated simply smashing his face into it. Eventually, he managed to flop one arm onto it and grasped a handful of fruit, which he promptly flung over one shoulder through a combination of poor aim and worse grip release.

On his second attempt, he punched himself in the mouth.

"I'll count that as a win," he said finally. "The aim was good."

"*A valid point,*" Prima agreed.

He eventually found a—mostly—viable strategy for eating. First, he would flop his arm onto the platter, then scrunch his hand around whatever was there. With food in his grasp, he'd flop the arm again and aim his palm at his face to try to get the food in.

Compared to the previous night's Prima-assisted meal, it was insanely messy.

"Is there a magical form of dry-cleaning?" he asked after he had eaten most of the food within range. He didn't think turning the platter was within the realm of possibility.

"Ah. Yes, one moment. Okay, now look at yourself. Wait! Don't try. I'll summon a mirror."

Ben studied his now clean countenance and was impressed. The game did, in some ways, know what he looked like, but it had also given him a cleaner shave than he'd ever managed to give himself. His eyes also seemed bluer than normal.

He wasn't bad looking, he reflected, and might even be good-looking enough for a certain elf to—

No. Bad thought. First of all, this was a game. Second, people were watching everything he did. Third, he still didn't know who the assassin was.

With a sigh, he considered his options, flopped both arms onto the table, and stood. This time, he was able to support himself with his hands so he didn't fall forward. He responded with a whoop of happiness, wondered if this was a big enough deal to get happy about, and decided he didn't care.

"Prima," he said, "it's time to try walking."

"Aww yiss," said the mechanical voice, followed by the sound of the chair scraping back across the floor to get out of his way.

Ben managed to get all the way to the door with only one fall, and he wasn't nearly as tired as he had been the day before. He was slowly finding a rhythm to the steps—or, perhaps, learning to reinterpret the pressure in his feet and legs. The result was that he didn't have to swing as wildly to shift a foot forward and his head didn't flop as much either.

At the door, he wobbled his torso and flung one arm out to

settle his hand on the doorknob. He was about to press it down when he remembered something.

"*Can you not get the handle to move?*" Prima asked. "*I checked. It's not locked.*"

"It isn't…that." He frowned, his hand still on the knob. "Zaara told me not to go anywhere." Mindful of how voices traveled out of the room, he kept his pitched low. "Although…I do want to try something."

Voices moved closer—two fae talking together, he decided. He couldn't hear footsteps as they didn't walk, of course, but he could tell that they were close. With all the speed he could muster, he shuffle-waddled sideways and pressed on the door handle enough to open the door. He lowered his hand to stop it, leaned against the wall—falling was still easy—and listened as he observed the passersby.

Their voices grew louder as they bobbed into view, and to his surprise, a very strange thing happened.

At the far side of the atrium his room adjoined, the two fae voices were suddenly magnified. He traced his gaze over the two crystal arches that supported the ceiling. They must be conducting the sound.

Which meant the two conspirators hadn't simply happened to be standing directly outside his room but had instead lurked near what did, in fact, appear to be an unused set of rooms.

That was sad. He had hoped they might be terminally stupid and thus easier to catch.

With a sigh, he lolled his head forward and threw it back and sideways to close the door. "Ow."

"*Do you think, perhaps,*" Prima suggested in an admirably level tone, "*that it might have been a flawed idea from the start?*

"None of that," he said with dignity. Then, with a sigh—his sighing skills had increased remarkably—he set off for the far side of the room once more. There was only one step that mattered, after all, and that was the next one.

"How's he doing?" Nick had, after waking up on the cot, run back to his apartment to get rid of his day and a half worth of stubble. He still yawned but now wore clean clothes and smelled like soap.

Amber could not describe how much of an improvement this was.

"He's doing incredibly well," she told him. "And we are seeing electrical impulses in the muscles he's using."

"There are certain things he won't get from the game," Dr. DuBois said as he wandered closer with yet another bag of popcorn. "A certain amount of strength, the bone density—of course—and *some* measure of balance and kinesthesia, although it will be impossible to know how much until we have him out again." He shook his head at the screen, his eyes wide. "I have to say, I expected this to work but I'm flabbergasted at how well it's working."

"I think part of it is that keeping him upright is easier without the constraints of…no magic," she pointed out. "Also, failure isn't as painful."

"That could be a barrier at some point," Nick reminded them.

"Yes, but right now, with as difficult as things are, I think a whole heap of bruises and concussions every time he missed a step would…maybe not be a great incentive to keep going."

Her partner nodded thoughtfully.

She looked at the doctor. "What do you think about taking him out at the end of the week?" she asked.

"It could be a good idea," the man said slowly, although he looked doubtful. "I find myself torn between two potential downsides. First, that it's not working and we take longer than we should to realize that. Or second, that it's working more slowly in real life than in the game, and if we take him out too soon, we'll mistake slower progress for no progress."

"And, of course, the more his muscles atrophy, the more diffi-cult it gets to apply his proprioception in real life," Nick added.

Amber nodded but held a finger up as she searched through the pile of forms on her desk. "Yes, but...look at this. His muscle tone in certain muscles has increased since he got in there."

He took the printout and raised an eyebrow at it. "His glutes? What, is he doing squats? If he is, I do not want to see that."

"The glutes are a postural muscle, dumbass." She twitched the paper away from him.

"Or maybe you like watching the squats," he suggested in a stage whisper.

She waved a hand at him to stop. "I'm very sure what you're suggesting is medical malpractice."

"You're not a medical professional," DuBois pointed out. "So I don't think it could be medical malpractice." At her glare, he backed away and hurried in another direction.

"You know..." Nick said slowly.

"*Don't*," she said, already anticipating the direction this was going in.

"I only intended to say that all of us could stand to get out of the lab more. I know Jacob was asked out by one of the lawyers upstairs."

"He was?" She looked quickly at Nick. The strength of her reaction surprised her. She and Jacob had dated in their freshman year at MIT, a relationship that had thankfully fizzled out before things got ugly, thus leaving them the possibility of remaining friends. She had never once, that she was aware of, missed dating Jacob.

And yet, there she was, suddenly annoyed that someone else had asked him out.

"You wouldn't know it from how much time he's spent in the lab," she said finally and decided to shut her mouth before she said anything else stupid.

Nick looked at her for a fraction of a second too long before he said, "Uh-huh."

"May I ask why you're not exploring?" Prima asked finally. *"I don't want to nudge you toward any particular course of action, but if you're hoping to find information in a timely manner—"*

"Zaara asked me to stay inside," Ben reminded her.

"Yes, and?"

"And while I do not entirely trust her, I would like *her* to trust *me.*"

"Oh." The AI seemed genuinely flabbergasted. *"So, you're doing something you don't want to do because you think she might...confide in you?"*

"Not on purpose. But if she doesn't think I'm a risk, she'll probably be more likely to let something slip." He tottered to a chair and half-fell into it. "That is if there's anything to slip about. Oof, I'm tired."

"Wow. I do not understand humans at all."

"Which is odd since your processors control a whole horde of characters."

"I didn't say I didn't make accurate characters. I said I didn't understand them."

Ben frowned. "What's the difference?"

"Any astronomer could chart the stars for you, but very few discovered why the planets seemed to move in the way they did. Being able to recreate a pattern is not the same as understanding it." She paused. *"Particularly when the pattern is based on rank insanity."*

"I'll have you know I take offense to that," he said with a grin.

"You may take offense to it but I dare you to refute it."

He was about to make a retort when there was a knock on the door. His gaze flicked upward. "We'll finish this later." To the door, he called, "Yes?"

It cracked open and Zaara peeked around it. She wore robes, today, of a pale color that shifted as she moved—sometimes pink and sometimes gold or gray. The coloring didn't suit her at all, he thought. She saw him study her and gave a half-hearted shrug as she stepped inside and sat on a nearby chair.

"I'm representing Insea during formal negotiations, so we all have to wear these fancy robes and tons of chains with different insignias. And *hats*." She shook her head. "The hats are the worst part. Anyway, I came to check on you and see if you needed anything."

"That's very nice of you," he said. "There's nothing in partic-ular I need." He looked around. "It is a little lackluster staying in these rooms, but at least I have my recovery to occupy me."

She winced in sympathy. "I'm sorry. I wish you'd come into the world someplace safer. How about this—if you can make it through today, I'll come and give you a primer on how to get around the palace without falling for any fae tricks. Then you can walk in the gardens and so on. Does that sound good?"

"Yes." Ben didn't have to feign his happiness. "Thank you. That would be wonderful."

"Excellent." Zaara stood and retrieved a hat that seemed to have short, half-stripped feathers protruding from it in every direction. She rolled her eyes, set the hat on her head, and left with a wave.

He waited for a few moments after the door was closed before he said, "I hope she's not the assassin. I'm starting to like her. Kural, now, seems like a bit of a douche."

"You have no idea," Prima said. *"I have to live with it twenty-four-seven."*

CHAPTER FIFTEEN

The long few hours while Zaara was gone stretched interminably. Ben walked from one side of the room to the other and back again until he knew the exact number of steps between each wall, each item of furniture, and each rug. Between walking sessions, he napped—and dreamed.

In his dreams, chalked fingertips clutched rough stone, sweat trickled down the small of his back, and the sun was bright on his skin. He could feel the stretch in his muscles as he reached up, his grip sure, and his fingers closed easily over tiny handholds in the rock.

But as always, those dreams ended with the sickening feeling of falling and the jerk against his harness. He startled awake with his heart pounding. Prima learned quickly not to speak to him after those moments. He would push up and start walking with grim determination.

He knew now what he needed—to be able to complete that climb. Until he did, the dreams would never go away.

Grimly, he ignored the voice in his head that constantly told him he might never recover enough for that.

Halfway through the day, however, Prima discovered another

way to distract him. He was part of the way across the floor when something appeared above the litter. It was an oblong shape that looked as if it was wrapped in liquid sunlight.

Ben stopped. "Prima, was that you? Or is it some fae trick?"

"Ah. Yes, that was me."

Now assured that he wouldn't inadvertently sign up for a life of servitude if he opened it, he wandered closer to study it. He was able to get his hand onto it with a reasonable level of skill, but the closest he could come to unwrapping it was scrunching his fingers.

It took a while and scratched at his rising irritation.

When the wrappings fell away at last and vanished before they hit the floor, he took a step back out of instinct.

It was a sword.

"Prima?"

"Yes?"

"Why is there a sword?"

"So you can learn to defend yourself," she said. *"Almost all who enter the game are given a method of combat. Obviously, we wanted you to get slightly more coordinated before we gave you sharp objects, but you're doing very well."*

"I don't want a sword," he objected.

"Would you prefer a staff? Daggers?"

"I don't want to do any crazy sword fighting stuff," he clarified. "I don't want to kill people. I told you that."

"Sometimes, circumstances will be out of your control," Prima responded calmly.

"This is a game! It isn't real and doesn't have to involve killing."

"It is a game that is designed to stimulate your fight or flight reflexes," she said flatly. *"That means we are testing not only deliberate movement but also the activation of your sympathetic nervous system. This is necessary."*

Ben folded his arms—or tried to—and glared at the ceiling.

He was about to make a retort when a rap came at the door and Zaara poked her head in again.

"Hi! Can I come in?"

He had almost fallen when he tried to turn and nodded. "Sure." He steadied himself and shuffled to a chair.

"Oh!" Zaara walked to the litter and looked at the sword, her eyes wide. "Where did you get this? You didn't have it when we first saw you. It wasn't delivered from someone, was it?"

"No, it's mine," he assured her. Trying to needle Prima, he added, "It's a family heirloom I'm trying to get rid of."

"You keep trying, buddy boy. See how that goes for you."

"You're trying to get rid of it?" Zaara gave him a wide-eyed look. She reached for the sword, then stopped. "May I touch it?"

"Go for it." He sat and watched as she picked it up and made a few passes in the air.

"It's not the best weapon I've ever held," she said finally, "but it's quite good—and I honestly think the balance problems could be corrected by a good blacksmith. I know one if you'd like me to bring you there when all this is over. Justin, Lyle, and I helped him when he was attacked by a demon army."

"A *demon* army?"

"A demon's army, not an army of demons," Zaara clarified. "The demon had found a magical stronghold and—well, it's not important."

"No, I want to hear." He raised an eyebrow. "Especially if this is the Justin whose world you think I'm from."

"Ah, right. That." She sat on the bed. "How about this. When we're done with the treaty, we'll have a long journey back and I'll tell you everything then. But you asking me if I was 'real' is something I've come across a few times, and it's always people from Justin's world who do it."

Ben chewed his lip. Zaara—or the pile of algorithms that made Zaara—drew conclusions from disparate pieces of data. He had known that Prima was becoming self-aware, but was Zaara?

She certainly didn't seem to know that she was part of a computer like Prima did.

Was she even distinct from the AI, though?

His philosophical musings were enough to give him a headache and he met her gaze with an apologetic shake of his head. "I was daydreaming, sorry."

"There's no need to apologize. I can tell you've been working hard at your recovery. Would you like me to come back later?"

"*No,*" he said emphatically. When her eyebrows rose at his vehemence, he added, "I'm *so* bored."

She laughed. "I know that feeling. Let's get you trained on fae tricks, then, so you can at least have a change of scenery every once in a while."

Zaara proceeded to give him an informal lecture on some of the common methods of trickery the fae used while he looked on in amusement. She was fascinated by the topic, but she was far from a natural teacher and her mind made intuitive leaps that she never quite explained.

She knew enough, however, to give him a quiz at the end. "So, what do you do if you're walking down a hallway and a door appears where there wasn't one before?"

"Never, ever open it," he said. This was apparently an important point as she had returned to it after almost every other item on the list.

"And if a door disappears where there was one?"

"You can find it by sniffing along the wall because the fae illusion will smell of ozone."

"Yes." Zaara smiled, pleased. "And then?"

"Then take a coin and toss it against where the spell is to see if there's any magic keeping things from passing through. If not, you can feel for the door and open it yourself. If so, you need to ask the fae who did the spell to appear and let you through."

She nodded and raised her eyebrows for the next part.

"They'll try to get me to do them a favor in return for giving the door back," he said.

"And so?"

"So I flip it by reminding them that they've done me a *disservice* by hiding the door and that what I owe them is to take something of theirs. As long as I hold to that point, they will eventually cave and show me the door if I'll agree not to take something they like."

"No, no," Zaara said. She shook her head. "You never agree to *anything*, remember. You merely hint that you'll have to until they give the door back. If they ask you for a promise, even if it sounds like that's what they're asking, there will be a trick in there."

Ben groaned. "This place is a nightmare."

"Kural thinks so," she agreed. She sat on the edge of the bed and toyed with her strange hat. "Sometimes, I think he's put out at not being the smartest one in the room, you know? Or that they use all their intelligence for the tricks. Fae are quite intelligent. Even the stupidest of them is likely to be smarter than most humans, and Kural prides himself on his mind."

"He sounds insufferable," he said bluntly.

She smiled in response. "Many people think so."

"And you don't?"

"Not...always." Her smile became rueful. "He has quite a good sense of humor usually, which you don't see right now, and he was kind to the people he ruled for hundreds of years. Wizards are notoriously cruel but he wasn't. He kept them safe and he spent time on his research. But..."

"But?"

"But there's another side to him." Zaara hunched her shoulders. "When he was defeated by Sephith, he was cursed—he couldn't use his powers or tell anyone who he was. So he would travel around, training people, sending them on quests, and trying to make them strong enough to defeat Sephith. Now, he was cruel and someone needed to deal with him, so I don't blame Kural for what he did. But I think he got used to using people, you know?"

Ben nodded. He had the sense to not say anything and interrupt her train of thought.

"He thought this whole trip was a waste of time," she told him. "The treaty, I mean. He complained all the way here, he's walked into stupid traps the fae set for him, and he constantly wants to call it all off and go home."

"And you think that would be the wrong thing to do," he said, exploring this unfamiliar territory.

"Yes." Zaara was emphatic. "I'm not saying we need to forge a grand, eternal friendship. Only something to start to build a relationship between Insea and the fae. The world is becoming less stable with more wars, more bandits, and more famines. If nations don't stand together, there will be war—and war is never how you want to resolve things."

He stared at her. "That's a strange sentiment from a woman who carries knives."

"One person with weapons is very different from armies and sieges," she said practically. "But also, I said it's never how you *want* to resolve things. I'm an emissary because I don't like wars and violence. I carry weapons because I know sometimes, those things happen anyway." Soberly, she added, "Some people don't dislike violence."

"I've met a few of those," Ben said quietly. She looked at him, interested, and he shrugged. "Where I come from, many people think…being a warrior is the greatest expression of what a man can be."

"How bizarre." Zaara tilted her head in thought. "One would think it is obvious that the world could not function if all people were warriors."

"I didn't say people," he reminded her, "I said men."

"Oh. Do women not become fighters where you are?"

"Not as often. But…not never, either." He shrugged. "There are some in every war."

"Huh." She considered this with a small frown. "But you say you have only ever met men who liked violence? Never women?"

"I suppose…I don't know. I can't think of any women who believe it's their destiny or anything like that. The men I know who like being violent…they like to dress it up like it's not something they can or should control."

Zaara frowned at him. "Haven't you ever wanted to lash out at someone? Someone who was being cruel or hurting others?"

Ben shook his head. "I…yes, of course. But that's not the way to solve anything."

She smiled. "What a strange world yours must be if you never have to use violence."

"No one ever *has* to use violence."

"Of course they don't." She was amused now. "Neither does anyone *have* to eat or breathe or read or help others. One can always choose to stand back…or fade away. But if you want to live and you want to do the right thing, you'll sometimes have to use different tactics."

He pondered this for a moment. It seemed as if she had accepted the necessity of violence, which was something that worried him as a quality in an ambassador. However, he was honest enough with himself to know that he could not see any particular flaw in her reasoning. There were bullies sometimes, people who forced fights.

Was he a realist who knew that schoolroom behaviors could be avoided in the real world? Or was he simply an idealist who wanted that to be true?

The thought ended abruptly when a gong rang through the entire palace—a chime that filled him with absolute dread.

"What was that?" he asked.

She leapt to her feet and tore her robes off to reveal the armor beneath. "I don't know but I know it's not good. Come on!"

CHAPTER SIXTEEN

Zaara raced into the hall, leaving Ben to totter behind her. The urgency of the situation seemed to have a paradoxical effect on his coordination, which meant he almost fell several times and eventually resorted to the exaggerated steps he had first used. Every shout and question he heard from the corridor only made him angrier.

He couldn't even manage the most basic parts of this game. Other people started with a sword and became legendary heroes. He played in easy mode and he couldn't even do that.

By the time he reached the hallway, the confrontation had moved toward the throne room and his anger had turned into self-loathing. The distance to the nearest intersection in the corridors looked impossibly far, and he knew it was barely halfway to the throne room.

Even if he managed it, he would have missed almost everything when he arrived. Still, driven by God only knew what urge, he began the trek. *One step at a time, Ben. One step at a time.*

Sometimes, he found a rhythm that helped him walk almost normally but noticing that almost always led to him messing up again. The awkward, exaggerated movements began to take a toll on the muscles in his back and legs.

Ben ached all over when he reached the throne room and steadied himself on the door frame while he looked up. The chamber again seemed impossibly large. He had the peeved thought that it was the kind of room invented by people who didn't have any problem moving.

Would it have done them any harm to squish things together more?

"Hello," a smooth voice said next to him. "What are we missing, do you think?"

His stomach dropped with a lurch and he looked at Yn'solde, who watched the chaos with amusement. As she had the day before, she managed to project elegance.

"I'm not sure what's going on," he told her. "I wasn't…able to get here fast enough." His cheeks burned with shame at having to talk about his injury.

"I was under the impression you could not walk at all," she said. "It seems I rather underestimated you." Her dark gaze was fastened on him with unsettling intensity.

"I…" He trailed off as he had no idea what to say to that.

Thankfully—and infuriatingly—Kural arrived. The wizard panted from the exertion of his run and his cheeks had turned a purplish hue. Even after a day spent getting used to it, the blue skin still looked absurd.

"What's going on?" he asked.

"We don't know," Ben said. "Zaara's in there somewhere." He wobbled his head vaguely in the direction of the hubbub at the front of the throne room.

Hubbub certainly seemed to be the best way to describe it. A tangle of fae tumbled over one another and all of them shrieked at the top of their lungs while Zaara, one of the humans, and the orc shielded their heads with their arms and yelled in return. The guards darted between the groups with their weapons drawn, which didn't seem to make anything better.

"Of course she is," Kural muttered, and he yanked Ben with him as he strode into the throne room.

Yn'solde appeared fortuitously on his other side. She took his arm—as if he were escorting her—but the pressure of her hand steadied him. He gave her a grateful look and she smiled. When the wizard charged into the fray, she held Ben back.

"I don't think anyone will be well served by us getting injured," she told him. She waited, her gaze tracing the group, then caught sight of his worried expression. "Oh, don't fear—almost everyone there is trained in combat. They can take care of themselves. The fae may present a rather childlike appearance to the larger races, but they're quite competent with weapons."

Ben, who had been deeply unsettled by the tiny fairies brandishing sharp pikes, took comfort from this.

"So, how did you come to be here?" he asked her. When she gave him a curious look, he had the sense that he had misstepped. "Apologies. You don't need to answer that."

"I'm merely surprised there is someone who doesn't already know the whole story." She gave him a somewhat bitter smile. "I'm the youngest in the family of Yn'sur."

"The…elven king," he said and scrabbled to remember what Zaara had told him.

Yn'solde, thankfully, mistook his ignorance for disbelief. "The same—if 'king' is a term you want to use. He always was single-minded about the things he wanted. I suppose we should have known that only ruling the world would satisfy him…if that."

"You left because you weren't on the best of terms," he guessed. It seemed to be a massive understatement, but he didn't want to make the situation sound salacious.

"Yn'sur always gets what he wants," the woman said. There was deep bitterness in her tone. "He has a talent for bending people to his will. I heard there was one human who defied him recently—and died in the attempt, apparently. She helped your friends in their quest to bargain with him." She nodded to Kural and Zaara, both of whom were still in the midst of the brawl. While they each appeared to be wounded, they didn't look upset about it.

Ben put the pieces together in his head. "So...they were ambassadors to him before they came here?"

"So it would seem. I don't know what bargain they struck with him in the end. Some news of his reign is inescapable, but I try to remain...free of it." She watched the brawl still but her gaze was distant.

"Are you in danger?" he asked her finally, mainly because he didn't know what else to say.

She frowned at him. "Of course I am," she said as if there was nothing surprising about it. "Anyone of royal blood is in danger at any time. You can try to run from it but it always finds you in the end."

As she spoke, the knot of fighters in front of the throne was driven apart by the guards, and Yn'solde fell silent. On one side of the divide were the fae, still yelling things that sounded like accusations, with all of the non-fae on the other side.

Ben began to limp toward Zaara and Kural but the elf held him in place with surprising strength.

"Don't get involved," she said quietly. "Whenever possible...do not get involved."

He hesitated. While he wanted to help Zaara and Kural—more the former than the latter—he had the sense that Yn'solde's advice had been learned the hard way. Also, what could he do that was useful? He wasn't a diplomat and he didn't have the faintest idea of what was going on.

The throne had been curtained, a feature he didn't notice until the drapes drew back from around it. Everyone seemed to hold their breath, but when the king became visible, the storm of accusations and yelling began again.

"Silence!" the king said. There was no particular vehemence to the word but strangely, it vibrated right into Ben's bones.

An immediate hush fell over the group.

"What is the meaning of this?" the monarch asked the assembled group.

Again, he had the useless urge to step forward, and again, Yn'solde held him back.

"We found this one!" one of the fae said. It flung an arm out at the human, who stumbled forward when the guards pushed him. Like his companion Ben had seen the night before, he had skin of a deep brown and black hair that was held back in an elaborate set of braids.

He wondered where his companion was—a question that was almost immediately answered.

"The other human was arrested," the fae trilled. "But he walked around free."

"Arrested?" Ben asked Yn'solde.

She shook her head and her face took on a watchful stillness. He wondered if she had seen this before—the accusations, the mobs, and the arrests.

"His companion was arrested," the king agreed, "for crimes committed. This human was not a party to her crimes and therefore has not been arrested."

"He is also suspect!" one of the fae called. "How could he not be a party to it all?"

"And there is a new human," another called. It twirled and pointed unerringly at Ben. Its face didn't look childlike now—or, if it did, it was like the possessed child from a horror movie. "This one arrived and that very night, another snuck into the king's chambers."

Another storm of yelling erupted, but he made out one accusation.

"And those two sheltered him."

The area around Ben, Zaara, Kural, and the other human

suddenly cleared. Even Yn'solde stepped aside and wouldn't meet his eyes. Disappointment and betrayal twisted in his chest while he tried to understand. She had fled her court because of bad politics. It made sense that she didn't want to stick her neck out.

All the same, her abandonment hurt.

He wouldn't do the same thing. With all eyes on him, he limped slowly to the throne. Kneeling was hard and he almost fell. It was the human he didn't know who helped him, offered a steadying hand, and stepped back.

"Light of the fae," Ben said, "I swear I have not known of or been a party to any crimes against you."

Even as he said it, he knew it was a lie. He knew someone was planning to kill this king, and when he looked up, disgust and anxiety choked him. Confusion and uncertainty swept over him, and he knew that if he did not do the right thing, the man he was looking at would be dead soon.

Something told him that spitting out everything he knew, here and now, would not help matters.

The king nodded but something in his eyes made him wonder if he sensed the lie.

"None of the humans here are convicted of any crimes," he said clearly. "Therefore, they are all still guests." *And I expect you to behave accordingly,* his tone said.

The crowd dispersed, still muttering, and a guard came to help him to his feet.

But when Ben stood, the point of a pike pressed against his ribs. The guard was smiling but his eyes were cold as he said, "Conspire with the others of your kind, human, and I'll gut you like a fish."

CHAPTER SEVENTEEN

The king's edict of hospitality was followed to the letter. Every guest was given a place to sit and food to eat.

It was very evident that the fae took pains to be very, very polite. There was no way to force genuine goodwill, however, and the members of the other races stayed only long enough to be courteous before they left. None of them spoke to each other as all of them worried that they would look suspicious. Ben did not even dare to thank the human who had helped him kneel at the foot of the throne.

When he left alone, he was very conscious of the gazes of the fae following him and of his awkward gait. At least, he thought with a certain wry humor, he wouldn't be suspected of being a light-footed assassin.

He was almost at his room when Zaara caught up with him. She must have waited quite a while after he left, and he noticed that she came from another direction—perhaps to throw the fae court off the scent.

She didn't speak in the hallway but ushered him into his room and shut the door behind them.

"What happened back there?" she asked him.

"Don't ask *me*. I missed most of it."

"No, I mean with the guard." She hesitated. "And…Yn'solde. I wouldn't trust her, Ben."

"Believe me, I know." He lurched to a chair and sat with a groan of relief. "She's out to save her hide and nothing more. She proved that."

Zaara made no reply to that. She sat in another chair and studied him for a moment.

"Oh, right. You wanted to know about the guard." He raised his eyebrows. "Garden variety threats, nothing more. I can see why not many other races settle here. They're not exactly friendly, are they?"

"They aren't, no." She sighed. "And the fact that they think of other beings as toys doesn't help. I wonder if that's why they're so angry. No one expects their pet to betray them."

"Why was the human sneaking around in the king's chambers?" he asked her.

"No one knows." She shrugged. "Well…none of the mob, certainly. And before you ask, I know that because they accused *me* of all kinds of things I didn't do. If they knew what she'd done, I assume I wouldn't be on the receiving end of that."

Ben watched her narrowly. If he trusted her, now would be the time to tell her what he had heard the night before. It seemed like too big a coincidence that a human woman had been arrested the same night he heard two women plotting against the king's life.

"What do you get out of peace?" he asked her finally. "Why are you here? Yn'solde said you bargained with her brother, too."

"She told you that, did she?" Zaara looked interested. "I wasn't sure she knew. She takes pains to stay away from any news of him. Although, having met the man twice, I can say I understand the urge. He's insufferable."

To test her, he said, "She said he always wanted to rule the whole world."

"He's well on his way to that," she agreed. Then she saw his face. "I keep forgetting you don't know what's going on here. Insea—the city I represent—was founded by the elves and was, until very recently, considered the elven center of power in the world. The dwarves make their home in Berghold, the orcs... well, no one has seen them for a long time, which is a whole story on its own, and the humans are always fractured between a host of kings and dukes and so on.

"Well, some of the elves decided they wanted more. Yn'sur—that's her brother—declared himself a monarch and has spent the past few years setting up a...kingdom, I guess you'd call it. It's not weird to me, given that I'm human and people declare themselves sovereign lords all the time, but the elves took it *very* seriously. Yn'sur probably has most of them behind him now, and he's rallying them all with the belief that elves are supposed to rule the entire world."

"Huh. And Yn'solde ran away because?"

"She and I haven't talked much," Zaara said. "She takes a very nihilistic view of the world, which is something I don't have the luxury of."

"As an ambassador," Ben said.

"Yes." She leaned back in her chair and one hand played absentmindedly with the empty scabbard at her waist. "I never wanted a normal life, you know—marriage, children... When Kural offered to make me his apprentice, everything seemed *right*. It was the status my family had always wanted, I'd be able to follow my interests, all of that. But..."

He watched her in silence.

She looked at him. "It's difficult to not be terrified of war when you know you'll live hundreds of years," she told him. "You start seeing it behind every corner. Kural is jaded—or maybe he never cared as much, I don't know. But I wanted to protect my family and I *believe* in this. If I'm going to protect them, I can't merely be a wizard in my tower, making sure the rains come on time. I have to make sure the whole world stays stable. War touches everyone."

"You want this to work," he said. "The treaty."

"Yes." She gave him a humorless smile. "Why, have you talked to Kural? Did he tell you I'm an idiot?"

"I haven't talked to him," he said. "I only know you think people are working against it."

"War is profitable," Zaara said simply. "That, and there are detractors at every court, people who want to hold out for a better offer of some other nefarious purpose. The king constantly delays making any formal agreement with us—anything at all. I don't understand it."

"Is there a faction at court trying to bring him down?" Ben asked her.

"You mean…a fae faction?"

"Anyone."

"I don't know. I guess I would assume so. There always is, isn't there?" Then, she saw his face. "Why?"

It all came down to this, he thought. This one judgment call. Could he trust her or did he merely *want* to?

He closed his eyes for a moment and willed Prima to make a suggestion, which she of course would not do. If he trusted Zaara and she was untrustworthy, the king would die—and possibly him as well.

If he didn't find an ally, however, the king would almost certainly die. Kural wasn't someone he would trust for a moment, and he wouldn't bet on Yn'solde to stick her neck out this far if she was so determined to stay away from political matters.

Which meant that if he trusted anyone, it had to be Zaara.

Resolute, he opened his eyes. "I heard two women outside last night," he confessed. "They were talking about killing the king."

Her jaw dropped and her mouth opened in a little O. "Are you *sure?*"

"Yes. One of them said she didn't want to so the other one would have to stall…something. I don't know what. The other one said there was no way to stall it anymore, and if she didn't want to kill him, she could simply *not* kill him. The first said if she hadn't agreed to it, she would have been killed and another assassin would have been sent in her place. Then the other one said she would do what she could, but the first one should stay away from her—she didn't want to be known as being involved in it."

Zaara had her hand over her mouth now.

"I don't know who it was," Ben said. "I couldn't get to the door fast enough." He nodded in that direction. "But I checked this morning—if you're on the opposite corner of the atrium, the sound carries very peculiarly into this room. They thought they were alone."

She looked at him, her face drawn. "And you didn't know if you could trust me," she said quietly. "You thought I might be one of the two voices."

For a moment, he thought she might draw her remaining dagger and stab him.

"I'm not," she said. "I wasn't. Is there any way I can prove it to you?"

"Probably not," he said honestly. "None I can think of right now. But I can't stop this on my own. I'm…" He looked bitterly at his body.

"You're vulnerable," she said bluntly.

He pressed his lips into a thin line.

Zaara stood decisively. "There's no time like the present to fix that." She strode to the litter and picked the sword up, flipped it haft-out, and extended it to him. "Get up. We'll teach you how to use this."

Ben gaped at her.

She gave him an unimpressed look. "Up. We don't have much time."

"Not if our strategy is 'make Ben the king's bodyguard,'" he agreed. "But that would be about the stupidest strategy I could come up with, even if you gave me a year to think about it."

"That is *not* my strategy," she said. "However, I still don't know who else *I* can trust. Some fae can shapeshift, there are people at court I still haven't met, and who knows what undercurrents are around us. I need to think and I think best while I fight. *You*, meanwhile, need to be at least partly capable of defending yourself."

He closed his fingers around the sword and stood. "Okay," he told her, "but I'll remind you that someone having a weapon they can't use is a *very bad idea*."

"That's why we'll teach you to use it," Zaara said as if explaining something to the terminally stupid.

With a grimace, he stood and tried a couple of passes with the sword but only narrowly avoided falling and made her skip out of range with alacrity.

"I don't want to kill anyone," he told her.

"I know you don't," she said. "But then you let the people who are willing to use violence control the world. I don't think, when push comes to shove, you'll want to do that." She smiled encouragingly at him. "And I don't think you'll be unsteady on your feet much longer, either. I think you'll be back in fighting shape soon. You don't have to use the sword, Ben. You're merely going to learn how in case you decide to."

"Fair enough." He would let that slide for now. If nothing else, he could use this as training for coordination. "What's the first lesson?"

"The first lesson," Zaara said, "is how to stand." She took her dagger, held it out, and settled her weight over her back leg. "You see? Legs apart, both feet pointed half-out. It's easy to shift weight or to move in any direction."

"Uh." Ben tried to copy the position and almost fell. "I think I should try this without the sword first."

"Nope." She was unequivocal. "You're learning how to move again, and you have a chance to learn that with a weapon in your hand. Most warriors would do anything for that chance."

"They can have it," he muttered. "I don't want it."

He was surprised by a thwack across his knee with the flat of her blade. She gave him a smile that sent his blood running cold.

"You have the hand you're dealt," she said simply. "And if you won't respond to gentle instruction, I'll have to do this the hard way."

"What's the hard way?" he asked, suddenly wide-eyed. "Did your...fencing instructor...hit you?"

"Not my fencing instructor," Zaara said. "My dancing instructor. She used a cane, of course, instead of a knife, but I can improvise. If you like, I can do things exactly how she did and throw in some personal insults as well."

"Um. No thanks." He had a sudden, intense desire to never learn any type of dance. "I'll be good. Don't hit me."

"Excellent. Now show me the stance again."

CHAPTER EIGHTEEN

Nick was about to head out for the night when Jacob arrived. Amber, in mid-shift, was deeply engrossed in a spreadsheet and didn't notice him—but he clearly noticed her. Nick saw his gaze trace the more carefully braided hair, the fitted t-shirt, and the new jeans.

Amber was Amber, after all. She wouldn't come to work in a dress and heels.

He watched surreptitiously out of the corner of his eye as the other man looked at his attire—a sweatshirt with a small stain on the edge of the pocket. He pulled the garment off, stuffed it behind his desk, and ran his fingers through his hair before he sat to turn his computer on.

Nick hid his smile in his cup of cocoa and pivoted in his chair to greet his friend.

"Is there anything I should know?" Jacob asked him.

"Nothing that I can think of," he said and added, "Amber might have something, though. I don't know. She's been at the monitors."

Jacob looked at her and his gaze lingered for a moment before he said. "Yeah, of course." He cleared his throat. "Uh...any plans tonight?"

"Did you just *meet* me? You know I'm terminally lame."

"I do. I know that." the man grinned. "I merely keep hoping *one* of us will take advantage of living in New York."

"I think Amber's going to a concert this weekend."

"Huh." He looked at her again. "Okay...well, I guess you're off the hook."

Nick shuffled his papers and made sure everything was in the handoff folder. Amber had been watching Taigan today while he watched Ben.

The truth was, with the team Diatek had helped them hire and the fact that both patients were stable, the members of the PIVOT team no longer needed to work eight hours on, eight hours off. They were certainly sleep-deprived and overworked enough that a break would do them good.

But working like this was a habit at this point. None of them had much going on outside work, and these two cases were interesting.

"So, I'm not sure how Taigan is," Nick told Jacob. "There were no emergencies, obviously. I'd have noticed that. Ben is doing well, though. He's probably one of the stubbornest people I've ever seen. He doesn't have to worry as much about overworking muscles since he's in the game—so he's basically doing PT twenty-four-seven."

"I saw the same thing," his friend said with a grimace. "The game has social aspects, too. Does he know that?"

"About that." He selected one of the papers. "I caught an interesting conversation between him and Zaara—oh, that's the big news I forgot. He's decided to trust her."

"*Finally*," Jacob said.

"In retrospect, we *did* throw him into a snake pit. Justin or Tina would have known to trust her but he had no clue."

The other man looked a little embarrassed. "I hadn't thought of that."

"Me, neither. Lesson learned for next time, I guess. Anyway, he and Zaara were talking and he brought up killing people again. He really, *really* doesn't like the idea." He frowned at the transcript before he passed it to his colleague. "I thought our holdouts would all be people like Dotty—and even she went with it."

Jacob made pondering noises as he read the details. He tapped his fingers on one leg. "I suppose we should have expected this. Killing people in a standard video game is very different than killing them all…up close and personal."

"It's not that, though." Nick frowned. "He hasn't even had the chance yet. It's not like he dislikes the experience. For him, it's a moral thing."

"Okay, there are people from all age groups who buy the 'video games cause violence' trope. In fact…" Jacob looked vaguely panicked. "I'm surprised we haven't had terrible publicity yet. Huh. Someone should tell Anna Price about that. But not me."

"If you didn't want to do things like this, you shouldn't have been CEO," Nick said.

"I went to jail for you people!" His friend jabbed a finger at him.

"Oh. Right." He had the sense that he had unequivocally lost this fight. "Anyway, it's something to consider. Dotty didn't like it but she got on board in certain instances. I don't know how Ben will do. We might want to start thinking outside the box on what could get that life-or-death response that *isn't* combat. I thought something like mountain climbing."

"Ah. Adventure treks, surviving against the elements." Jacob nodded. "Not for Ben, though."

"Yeah…"

"What are you two talking about?" Amber asked. She wandered away from her monitors with a fresh cup of tea.

"Ben not wanting to get into the more, ah…stabby…parts of the game," Nick explained.

"If I couldn't walk well, I wouldn't want to try to use a weapon, either." She took a sip of tea. "Well. Maybe a flamethrower."

Every so often, he was reminded to not mess with her. This was one of those moments.

"How's Taigan?" Jacob asked her.

"Great. She and Prima have good conversations and she's learning to hold onto her appearance," she said and sat on one of the stools. "Um…what else? Not much. It's slow going, exactly like Ben. She's not even ready to be in the game world yet."

"It's weird how much we're learning from each of the patients." Jacob leaned back in his chair. "If you'd asked me if someone could lose their sense of self enough to not even project a character image in-game, I'd have said no. But there are all these things we built the game around that were testing unin- jured people."

His companions nodded.

"I think the thing to hold onto is that it's *working*," Amber said. "It's a gentle way to bring people back to the world. I read some- thing a while back—that the goal of virtual reality or technolog- ical upgrades is to be better not only when you use them but also when you stop. I think we are doing that."

The other two nodded at her and Nick smiled slightly. "I'm gonna head out. Call me if you need anything."

"Sure," she said. Beside her, Jacob nodded.

He was grinning as he left the lab. The other two were in close-headed discussion. His plan was working.

Of course, he knew the truth would come out eventually. He could deny it and say it was a misunderstanding but they would discover that he'd made up the story about Jacob being asked out by one of the Diatek lawyers.

It wasn't that they'd purposefully fought their feelings for each other. They were simply two of the most oblivious people he knew. They needed the nudge. He merely had to hope that by the time they discovered his subterfuge, they'd be happy enough together that they wouldn't kill him.

Just in case, though, he should live it up while he still had the chance. That meant dim sum. He zipped his coat and whistled a cheerful tune as he pushed out of the building.

Taigan woke to the same blue she had seen for the past few days.

And one new thing.

She pushed up and stared at the door. "Prima?"

"Yes?"

"What…is that?" The door looked like one you might find in any eighties or nineties condo, the kind of hollow, faux-wood, white-painted door that always had a few scuffs around the edges. It and the white door frame were set incongruously in the middle of absolutely nothing.

"I assume you are not speaking literally. It is a physical manifestation of the entrance to a new part of the game." Prima sounded pleased. *"For the past two sleep cycles, you have kept your physical projection intact. You are ready to interact with more pieces of the game."*

"I am?" She curled in a ball.

"I am not perfect at interpreting human emotions. I sense that you are scared. Is that correct?"

"Yes, that's correct." She tried to keep from rolling her eyes and wasn't *annoyed* at Prima. The eye-roll would be affectionate. But she wasn't sure she would know that. "I like this place. Can't I stay here?"

The AI paused for a moment. *"No,"* she said finally. *"The point of this exercise is to wake you up."*

"I'm not ready to wake up." She had no idea how she knew that. In fact, up until that came out of her mouth, she would have said she was desperate to get out of there.

"You don't have to wake up yet," Prima said gently. *"That is still a long way off. There are many stages to go through before you get there, I promise. The timeline will adjust to where you are."*

Taigan swallowed. "Okay, then." She stood, and—before she could give herself time to think about why she was uncomfortable—walked to the door and pushed it open.

"Are all humans this impulsive?" the AI asked curiously. *"Or is it only those I've had the pleasure to come across?"*

The girl didn't respond. Instead, she gazed at her surroundings in absolute awe.

She stood in a redwood forest. The air around her was heavy with moisture and the scent of greenery. Pine needles and leaves crunched beneath her feet and sunlight shifted in dappled patterns on the ground.

After a long moment of disbelief, she drew a deep breath and burst into tears.

"Taigan? Are you hurt? Is something wrong?"

The girl sat abruptly, wrapped her arms around her knees, and buried her face in one elbow. She rocked slowly the way she used to when she was little and was scared of going to sleep for fear that she would fall into a coma.

Although she had not wanted to come here, this place was perfect. In her sleep and her blue nothingness, she had forgotten that all this existed—trees and smells and sunlight.

The sobs grew worse before they got better and exploded out of her throat, raw and aching. Taigan pressed a hand against her aching stomach and covered her face with her other hand. She didn't know why she was crying. Part of it was fear—of something that hadn't happened or maybe of dying without ever coming back to someplace like this. Part of it was something else, though, and she couldn't name it.

It took a long time for the storm of tears to end and when it did, Taigan curled on her side on the forest floor and watched the light shift for a while. Slowly, she stretched one arm and felt the sunlight on her palm, then rolled onto her back and closed her eyes to allow the light to play over her closed lids.

"Prima?"

"*Yes?*" The AI sounded subdued.

"I'm okay," she assured her. "I'm sorry if I scared you."

"*Did I do something wrong?*"

"No." She smiled, still enjoying the sounds of the forest and the simplicity of lying there. "Sometimes, we don't know how much we wanted something until we get it. Nature has a way of healing."

Prima considered this in silence.

"So." Taigan sat and braced herself on her arms. "What am I supposed to do here?"

"*Nothing in particular,*" the AI said but still sounded unsure of herself. *It's merely an area for you to explore, get an idea of relational distances again, changing conditions, sensory input, that kind of thing.*"

"Oh." She stood and brushed her pants off. "Explore. I can do that." She held a hand out and visualized a bottle of water, which promptly appeared. With a smile, she lifted it and drank from it before she returned it to non-existence.

Prima did not initiate conversation while the girl walked around the forest. The enormity of the trees hid the hills and dips in the ground and she made as many games out of it as she could, jumping over gullies and balancing along roots and fallen branches.

It was a child's dream of a forest. Soft moss brushed her fingertips and boulders were perfect to scramble up. She found sticks that would make ideal swords and guns for her career as an imaginary pirate. As she fake-fenced her way along a gulley, she sensed Prima's good-natured laughter in the way the wind rustled through the bushes and leaves.

At no point did she feel fear. There was nothing there that would hurt her, she knew that for a fact. She was safe.

"Prima, how long can I stay here?"

"As long as you want."

Taigan smiled at the sky. "Thanks, Prima."

"You're welcome. But out of curiosity, can I expect crying as a reaction to good transitions?"

"Yep." She scrambled up a boulder.

"Interesting. Okay."

CHAPTER NINETEEN

By the time Ben had finished his first swordsmanship lesson, every muscle in his body ached. He hadn't even known he *had* muscles on the tops of his feet and the fronts of his shins, much less tiny and very specific muscles that ran along his sides. It didn't seem fair that he should find out about them now because they hurt so much.

None of this was even *real*, he thought grumpily.

Also, he was ravenous.

Several fae servants had come in silently with food and withdrawn before he or Zaara could ask for anything else. It seemed they were aware of the current opinion toward foreigners.

He looked at the food in embarrassment. "I don't suppose you'd consider eating in your room? No disrespect. It's only that it's an awkward process for me to eat and I'd prefer it if no one saw it."

From the look on her face, Zaara was picturing what that would look like. He saw the corner of her mouth twitch before she nodded at him.

"I'll check on you in the morning," she said.

"Is that wise if they all suspect us of…whatever it was?"

"They know you're my cousin and I'm rehabilitating you," she pointed out. "I think it would be weirder to not come see you. As much as I can, I'll behave as if everything's normal. It's the best way I've found to make people stop being stuck up and strange."

"Ah. And what are you planning to do about…" He raised his eyebrows meaningfully.

"Nothing," Zaara said promptly.

"Nothing?"

"Not yet. I haven't the faintest idea what to do yet, and we know our assassin doesn't *want* to carry out the killing. I'll try to discover what's going on in the court with a new eye, but moving hastily would be worse than doing nothing at this juncture." She shrugged. "It seems like the kind of thing that should have immediate action, but you *always* have to choose the timing of your battles. You can't do that until you know who you're fighting."

She disappeared with a last smile and Ben sat to eat. He managed the small potatoes and tiny dumplings, although melon slices and flatbread proved to be beyond him at this juncture.

Drinking water, meanwhile, was much more of a challenge. To do it, he had to try to sip out of a full glass, attempt to get as much in his mouth as possible when he threw a glass of water at his face, or—finally—pour the water into an empty bowl and plunge his face into it.

He was very, very glad that Zaara had not been there to see it.

"*I have to say,*" Prima commented after the meal, "*humans are endlessly inventive.*"

"How did you expect me to eat?"

"*The normal way. I assumed if you needed help, you'd tell me.*"

"Son of a—" He tried to throw his hands up and only managed to flail vaguely. "Okay, what now?"

"*Well, it's nighttime. I'm given to understand that humans either sleep at this time or do things they don't want people to know about.*"

Ben, who had been looking at the bed, paused and looked up with interest. "Things like what?"

"You'd know more than I would. I was merely observing."

He highly doubted that, and he also doubted that it had simply been an off-the-cuff commentary on human nature. His interest stirred, he leaned back in his chair and thought her statement through. Things he didn't want people to know about seemed to be particularly significant.

One thought came to him quite quickly. There were originally two, but one was a wildly bad idea, so he discarded it out of hand. The other was also risky but at least useful.

"Prima, can you give me a map of the palace, or is there one in the room somewhere?"

"There's one on the floor."

"On the…what?"

When he looked down, Ben saw that the ornate pattern on the floor—which he had thought was simply decorative—was a blueprint of sorts. He lurched out of his chair with fairly minimal fuss —he was getting better at this—and tried to position himself.

The throne room was the easiest place to start, and it lay beside the bed. He shuffled to it like a zombie and hobbled in a slow circle. Now that he was there, he realized that the throne room was only part of a far more massive area. The king's chambers must lie behind the royal audience chamber and he could barely imagine how open and airy they were.

Or how long it would take him to get across them.

If he started in the throne room, he could work back to locate his room.

He took a few awkward, halting steps to the cross-corridor he knew, turned, and identified his rooms as being somewhere under the litter, which was still next to the bed.

Now he knew where *he* was. The question was, where were the dungeons?

"Prima, are there other floors that aren't on this map?"

"The entire palace is on one floor," she clarified.

"Interesting. Thank you."

"You're welcome. May I ask what you're looking for?"

Ben considered this. Part of him wanted to keep her in the dark in the same way she'd kept him in the dark. On the other hand, not only would her knowledge be useful but he also wanted to horrify her.

"The dungeons where the human woman is being held."

A very long silence followed before she said, *"You're throwing caution to the winds, I see."* Prima's tone was dry.

"Yup, that's about the size of it."

"Ah. Well, I wish you luck."

"Thank you." He resolutely ignored the warning in her tone. "The question is…where are the dungeons? They are usually somewhere difficult to get out of, but there's only one floor…" He shuffled along until he found a section of the palace that was at the far end, tied to the rest of it only by a thin corridor. "I don't suppose you could tell me if that's the right place," he said to Prima.

"I'm torn. On the one hand, I don't want you to get arrested. On the other…"

"On the other you do?"

"No, I haven't the faintest clue what to say to you to make you stay here."

"Prima. Is that or isn't that the dungeons?"

"It is," she said and sounded sulky.

"Excellent. Thank you." He took a couple of steps toward the door and found a sudden weight on his back. "What the—*Prima.*"

The sword was sheathed there.

"What?" she asked far too innocently.

"I won't use it."

"That's fine. At least you'll have it."

With the sense of being told to wear a coat outside in the winter, he headed to the door with an eye-roll.

He had always been good at following maps, a skill that had served him well in his many years of camping and outdoor work.

It wasn't difficult to remember the twists and turns that led to the area of the palace designated as the dungeons. The only real challenge was walking, and he had begun to improve at that every time he tried. He almost looked like a normal human now instead of a zombie.

The fae did not seem to be nocturnal—or, if they were, they were frolicking in a meadow or something. The palace itself, however, was quiet. He limped along and focused on being quiet, which added a layer of difficulty to the task of walking.

Once he reached the prison section, it was very clear that this was not a friendly place. The crystal that formed the palace was carved into brambles and jagged branches that looked as if they were rotting away. Moonlight had shined into the rest of the building but there, it was dark and quiet.

Except for the fae, who all seemed to glow from within. He drew into the shadows to watch the guards on their rounds. Two watched the door into the dungeons, although they did less guarding and more drinking, it seemed. While he watched, they settled down to a game of dice.

"They're distracted," Prima said.

"Not distracted enough to sneak past them,"

"Sneak, no. But there are other ways."

Ben looked over his shoulder at the sword. He knew exactly what she was suggesting but he wouldn't do it merely because it would be convenient in the short-term. Besides, he had no idea what kind of hell that would unleash once the dead fae were discovered.

He waited as the fae grew horribly drunk and at last, both began to snore. Although he had no idea how much time had passed, he knew it was now or never. If there was a changing of the guard, he would have missed his moment.

With great care to stay quiet, he shuffled past them—much like an aging and unsteady speed-walker—and arrived in the prison area.

This part turned out to be incredibly easy, as there was only one cell. The fae, he thought, must not have much of a problem with crime. It took him a few moments in the dark to discern the form of a human. A moment later, he saw the flash of her eyes.

She was awake and knew he was here.

Ben hurried closer to her. "Hello."

"Insea's new pet human." She sounded amused. "What can I do for you?"

"I'm looking for...I don't know." He sighed. "Why did you get arrested?"

"I was caught sneaking into the king's chambers," she said promptly. She didn't seem inclined to try to avoid questions.

"Yes, but *why?*"

"My business is my own," she told him. She was infuriatingly calm and leaned against the crystal wall of the cell with one leg crossed over the other. "Why should it concern you?"

"Because I arrived in the middle of what *looks* like a very calm, out of the way court," he said, "but which is *actually* a weird... ocean of...I don't know. I'm not good with metaphors but there are many dangerous people here."

That seemed to amuse her. "Of course there are. Haven't you ever been to a court before? There are always dangerous people. Sometimes, they're assassins. At other times, they're simply courtiers who are willing to do anything to get ahead."

"Which one of those are you?" Ben asked boldly.

The woman raised an eyebrow. "What's it to you?"

"Well, for one thing, all the fae are accusing any other foreigner of being in league with you."

"We both know you're not," she pointed out, "and you being here will hardly help that impression. So why did you come?"

"Because I'm not very good at this," he said flatly.

"I can't argue with that." She examined her nails. "So. Have you decided to throw yourself clear of the sinking ship? Is that it?"

"What sinking ship?"

She only looked at him.

Ben thought furiously. She hadn't been there when he was arm in arm with Yn'solde, so that would mean… "Kural and Zaara? The peace treaty?"

The human nodded once.

"Why do you think that's a sinking ship?" he asked slowly.

"I don't think so, I know so—and I'm not the only one. That wizard of yours isn't taking it well. If it were up to him, I think he'd be long gone by now. He knows the dangers." She folded her arms. "The girl, though, is too idealistic for her own good. She won't make it through the training, mark my words."

"What training? To be a wizard? Why?"

She nodded. "For better or for worse, those who survive know how to look out for themselves first. Kural knows how to do that. She doesn't." She saw the look on his face. "It's nothing personal. I'm not *glad* she'll die. I'm merely saying she *will.*"

"You don't seem sad, either," Ben said. He was getting angry and he wasn't quite sure why.

"If I got sad every time someone went to an avoidable death, I'd spend all day crying." She shrugged. "There isn't time."

"So what is there time for?" He crouched to peer at her through the bars. It was only when he wobbled on his feet that he realized what he had managed to do and he had to clutch the bars to steady himself.

"How did you get injured?" she asked him. "What kind of injury robs a man of his ability to walk but doesn't injure his legs?"

"That's none of your business. What were *you* willing to get caught for?" He narrowed his eyes. "You claim to not believe in anything and that Zaara's a fool for being an idealist. While you like to play it off like you don't care, you're in a bad way. You stuck your neck out and did something dangerous. *Why?*"

The woman didn't answer for a long time. Finally, she said, "If

I were you, human, I'd save my own neck. You might be Zaara's family but you can't save her, she can't save you, and that wizard won't save either of you when push comes to shove. Get out of here if you hope to escape with your head still attached to your body."

Ben stared at her. "Don't you want help? Aren't you scared?"

"You're wasting your time," she told him simply. "And if you don't have the good sense to get out of here before someone catches you, that's your business. But I won't waste my time getting to know a dead man."

She turned over and went to sleep, leaving him staring at her for a few moments.

But he knew he wouldn't get any more out of her. With an annoyed shake of his head, he started back to his rooms, moving as quickly and quietly as he could.

At least she had one piece of good advice—to save his own skin. It bothered him more than he could say, however, to hear that. Yn'solde might have left him alone to face the scrutiny of the court and saved herself, but it seemed worse, somehow, that the human urged him to do the same instead of helping her.

Who was so resigned to a world without friendship or help that they would do something like that?

He wasn't sure he wanted to know the answer.

CHAPTER TWENTY

The next morning, Ben was waiting when Zaara arrived.

She raised her eyebrows to see him seated and ready with the sword across his knees. "Are you so eager to practice?"

"Think of it as coordination practice, not assassin training," he said sourly. "First, though—how sure are you that we can't be overheard here?"

"Very," she said flatly. She fished a pendant out of her armor. "I carry the spells with me."

"Ah. Well, that would work." He considered her assurance for a moment and nodded. "I went to speak to the human who was arrested."

"You *what?*" She looked horrified. "Ben, they already thought all the foreigners were suspect—"

"No one saw me," he insisted. "I snuck in."

"You, ah…" Zaara tried not to look doubtful.

"I am getting *much* better at walking." He couldn't help but feel slightly peeved. "You said so yourself. And no one was around last night."

"Mmm, yes—the fae tend to flit off in the meadows at night." She sat abruptly. "Are you sure no one saw you?"

"Very—look, we don't have time to focus on that. Things are…not good. She said she knows the negotiations will fail and that Kural knows it, too."

"Kural is a pessimist," she said. "He's been very open about the fact that he didn't expect this to work. It hasn't done us any favors, honestly."

"It wasn't…" Ben scratched the side of his head, then paused to look happily at his hand. "Hey, look! I did it!"

Zaara gave him an amused nod.

"Anyway, it didn't sound like that was what she was saying. I asked why she thought the negotiations would fail, and she said she didn't *think* so, she *knew* so, and so did Kural. And…well, never mind."

She stared into the middle distance, her gaze shifting as she put things together in her mind, but she looked at him at the last part. "What? And what?"

"She had some unflattering things to say about idealistic people," Ben said. "It's not important."

Zaara looked like she doubted that very much, but her attention was still on the more disturbing part. She considered for a long time, moved to the windows and paced, and spun her remaining dagger around one finger.

"What did she say about idealistic people?" she asked finally.

Ben knew he wouldn't get out of this without telling her. She was a singularly stubborn woman. He sighed and repeated the other woman's assessment of Kural as someone who would save himself over others, and her as an idealist who wouldn't survive her training.

Thankfully, she seemed more amused than anything else. She rolled her eyes. "Why do I get the feeling that this concept of *all* wizards is based on one or two she met? If Kural were only out for himself, he wouldn't have been the kind of leader he was. He's not a cruel man."

Ben hated to break her heart, but he needed to. "She didn't say he was cruel. She said that when push came to shove, he'd save himself rather than stick his neck out for us."

Zaara's expression told him he'd struck a nerve. She sat hard on the bed, her shoulders slightly hunched, and looked genuinely miserable now.

"You've known for a while that Kural wasn't helping negotiations," he said quietly. "Is it possible he's somehow involved in the assassination plot?"

"Or that he knows and he's not stopping it," she said. She might hate this but she didn't shy away from what it meant. With a grimace, she sighed and straightened a little. "You said you heard two women. Some fae can shapeshift and Kural probably can as well, but you said one of them told the other to stay away and not be linked publicly, which suggests they were both in their normal forms. The only explanation I can come up with is that it was Alia—that's the human woman you spoke to—and Yn'solde. They're the only two non-fae women here apart from me. And I know it wasn't me."

"Why would Yn'solde do something like this?" he asked with a frown.

"It depends which one she is," Zaara pointed out. "Is she the assassin or the other one?"

He swore and rubbed his head. "I wish I'd been able to get to the door in time to see them."

"I'm glad you weren't," she said. "People who sign up to assassinate heads of state don't take kindly to eavesdroppers. You would probably have had your throat slit, which wouldn't have helped anyone."

"At least then we'd know who was who, though. I'd say Alia was the assassin because she snuck into the king's chambers, but..." He tipped his head back with a groan. "And what are they trying to stall? If Alia's involved, then from her comments, it sounds like they were trying to stall the negotiations. Or maybe not since she's so sure those are going nowhere. Unless she's sure of it because she knows the king will be assassinated? Ugh, this is a nightmare."

Zaara nodded with a scowl, then looked up sharply. "And she said Kural knew the negotiations were going nowhere. Does he know it for the same reason?"

"Don't ask *me*. You're the one who knows him." He shrugged helplessly.

"Fuck," she said succinctly and lowered her head into her hands. "Fuck, fuck, fuck."

"So I assume you didn't come up with a way to stop all this," he said.

The look she gave him could have frozen lava.

Ben sighed and tapped his fingers on the sword as he thought. "You know, it might be good if he's involved."

"*Why?*"

"Because, unlike with other random people, we have a hope of persuading him." He gave her a level look. "Well…you do. I don't think I do."

"He doesn't listen to me," Zaara said.

"I think he does," he countered thoughtfully. "Alia said he would have cut and run if it were up to him—but he hasn't, has he? So he must be listening to you."

"It's not only that." She sighed. "There's so much resting on these negotiations. They *can't* fail."

"Huh." Ben watched her for a moment, but she didn't seem interested in explaining further. "Well then, it seems our best bet is to find out if he is involved. If he is, we'll have a better idea of what to do next—especially if you can get the whole plan out of him."

She nodded. "He's conversing with some of their wizards today so he'll be out of his rooms. We could look through them and see if there's anything damning."

"That sounds good." He leaned the sword against the chair and stood. "Let's go."

"Aren't you forgetting something?" She nodded to the weapon.

"I'm not bringing that."

"Yes, you are, or you're not coming at all. And before you ask how I can stop you, do you even know where Kural's rooms are?"

"I...no." Ben muttered under his breath as he picked the sword up. "But this is bullshit, for the record."

"Uh-huh." Zaara didn't seem particularly worried by his assessment. "Well, get ready, because we'll practice that bullshit again when we get back."

"You're very hopeful about us accomplishing this without being gruesomely killed."

"What can I say? I'm an optimist." She gave him a smile with more teeth than were necessary. "And our odds of not being gruesomely killed are better when we're both armed."

He rolled his eyes and limped to where she held the door open for him.

CHAPTER TWENTY-ONE

"How did you get into the dungeon, anyway?" Zaara asked quietly as they walked. She had thrown an illusion over them that hid his sword, and she kept one hand under his forearm, the very picture of a solicitous healer.

Ben, aware that they were being watched, didn't try as hard as he usually did to walk gracefully. He allowed himself to stumble and limp and even played up some of those moments. Even three days before, this level of coordination would have been entirely beyond him and he was proud of what he had managed to learn.

He took his time before responding as several fae came around one corner and flitted past them. They turned their tiny noses up at the two humans, and he got the sense that they were very pleased with themselves for the snub.

"I merely waited for the guards to pass out drunk," he told her when the coast was clear.

"Ah. So guards everywhere are the same." She flashed him a smile.

The palace by daylight was truly gorgeous, something he hadn't had the focus to look at before. The floor looked as if it had grown like a giant honeycomb, each hexagon filled with a pane of glittering crystal. The sunlight refracted into rainbows everywhere, and each beautiful archway reminded him of the impossibility this building would be in any other world.

It was a shame that it was home to a group of petulant toddlers—smart, grudge-holding toddlers with magical powers, no less.

They were a few halls away when they ran into Alia's companion. He walked aimlessly and he looked as if he hadn't slept well in days. Ben wondered if he was her partner, friend, or if he was a brother. It was difficult to tell.

He stopped when he saw them but didn't seem to know what to do next.

"Good morning, Trin," Zaara said gently.

"Good morning." He looked grateful and also desperate for someone to talk to.

"Thank you," Ben told him. "You helped me in front of the throne and I was not able to thank you that night."

"Of course," Trin responded with a small, sad smile. "I hope the court has accepted your innocence."

He gave him a wry smile in return. "Maybe someday." He didn't know what else to say. Was Trin innocent or was he in on whatever Alia had done?

Zaara swooped in with aplomb to save the day. "Will we see you tonight at dinner?" she asked the man.

"I, ah…yes. I think so. That is if I'm allowed. And if…" He looked over his shoulder in the direction of the dungeons.

It occurred to Ben that they should perhaps ask him questions about Alia, but he didn't know where to begin. That aside, with the man looking so miserable at the prospect of the woman's potential execution, it seemed in poor taste. He snuck a glance at Zaara, who shook her head.

She laid a gentle hand on Trin's arm. "Don't borrow trouble," she told him gently.

He swallowed and nodded. "I'll let you two go." He looked at Ben. "It's good to see you walking again."

"Thank you." He nodded to him and limped away with Zaara, who kept her mouth resolutely shut until they rounded a corner into a wing of the palace that had a blue tint to it. She led him to a set of double doors and knocked on them, then waited patiently.

Ben glanced at her, confused.

As a group of fae passed, she knocked on the door again. "Kural?" She opened it and peeked her head inside. "Hello. I have Ben with me. Can we come in?" She led him into the empty room and gave him a sly smile. "Appearances," she said simply.

"Sneaky." He looked around. "So…what are we looking for?"

"Anything, really." She shook her head. "I can't see him being stupid about something like this, but I think I have to accept that I don't honestly know what he's up to. Anything that's iron would be particularly noteworthy, as it's immune to magic."

He nodded and began to poke around the room. The bed had been left messy and the whole space looked as if no servants had been there in a while. He wondered if it was a purposeful strike or if the wizard had asked to be left alone.

"So, why are these negotiations so important?" he asked as he lowered himself carefully to the floor to look under the bed. After some awkward scrabbling at the covers, he realized the bed base was solid and nothing would be hidden under it.

Zaara didn't answer the question. She came to help him lever the mattress up, but they found nothing there.

As she didn't seem inclined to answer that question, he decided to try one of the other topics he was curious about. "Will Alia be executed?"

"I don't know." She paused to look over her shoulder at him and seemed genuinely worried. "I don't think she's a representative of any of the human governments. I think she and Trin are refugees. It puts her in a strange position."

"I still don't get why she did it," he muttered and limped to a chair that had been dragged close to the fireplace.

"She didn't tell you what she was trying to do?"

"No. She said her business was her own." He felt around the cushion and along the back of the chair. "I don't get it. She likes to talk a big game about not caring about anything, but if she doesn't care, why bother to do something so dangerous? You're right, it's probably her and Yn'solde. I simply don't understand it."

Zaara shrugged. "I've never met someone who wouldn't resort to unwise action if the right motivators were pushed. Everyone has them."

"You never seem surprised by anything, did you know that?"

"Wrong. I was very surprised by your accusations against Kural."

"Oh. Right." He grinned at her. "So, does this count as your version of unwise action?"

She gave him a severe look that nonetheless made her mouth twitch at the edges. "Yes. Why do you ask?"

"I'm curious." On a hunch, he sat in the chair.

"What are you doing? Kural won't be gone for too long."

"I'm checking something." He stretched his arms and waved them. A side table was within reach and he examined it before he opened a drawer. It took a few attempts to get it open, but when it looked inside, he saw a slim iron box. "Zaara, look at this."

She hurried closer to look and sucked in her breath. "Oh, no. Okay, let me try to get this open." She pulled a set of lockpicks out and began to work the lock, muttering to herself as she did so.

"Do you know how to do *everything*?"

"Most things," she said absentmindedly. "I can also make a good seating chart for a banquet, plan a household's food supplies for a year to within one bag of flour, and re-shoe a horse in a pinch. Learning things is fun, even when the thing you're learning is boring." She caught him looking at her. "What?"

Ben shook his head.

He had never met someone like Zaara. In some ways, she reminded him of himself. She was expected to do many things she did not want to do but hadn't run from her obligations. Instead of simply leaving, she had found another way to bring honor and safety to her family. Even when learning things she did not want to know, she had found joy in the learning and in turning those pieces of information into something she could use.

Unfortunately, he was very aware that he hadn't done as well in his life. His family didn't need him for income or security, but he hadn't been around for them in *any* way. He knew his parents had wanted him to check in more often, to be around, to have dinners with them, and to be a part of their community. His friends had missed him and had tried to help him.

In his obdurate way, he had blown all of them off.

The box clicked and interrupted his depressing train of thoughts, and he leaned forward eagerly to look as Zaara opened the lid. She leaned back as if she expected a booby trap of some sort.

There was no danger within, but there was a set of papers, many marked in a surprisingly tight script. She pulled them out and spread them over the bed.

"What are they?" Ben asked.

She bit her lip. "Research on the fae," she said. He could tell from the way she said it that there was more. "Some is from years ago and some isn't his work. But a few are recent—since we've been here. He's been taking notes on…"

"On?"

"The king," she whispered. She sat back on her heels and pressed her hands against her eyes.

He limped to her as quickly as he could. It was awkward to put a hand on her shoulder, but she gave him a grateful look anyway.

"It doesn't mean anything," he said. "Not necessarily."

"It's about the king's weaknesses and how he's bound to the land." She looked at him. "Why would he have this if it wasn't to kill him?"

"And why would he have sent Alia if he knew all this?" he countered. Briefly, he reflected on how strange it was that they had switched places.

"I don't know, but why would he hold it in an iron box if he didn't want it to be secret?" Zaara shook the papers at him.

He was trying to come up with an answer when one of her pendants flared.

"Shit!" She snatched the papers and stuffed them into the box. "Get to the outside doors—go now. He's coming back."

Ben limped to the windows, acutely aware of the fact that he couldn't run. He heard her put the box in the drawer and in the next moment, she slid under his arm and helped him. The noise from her pendant grew steadily louder.

She studied the play of shadows on the door to the balcony, then opened it and ushered him through. A touch on the pendant quieted it, and she hastened out with him before she closed the door softly behind them. She guided him to the very edge of the platform and touched one finger to her lips to tell him to be quiet.

They heard the door open and Kural walked into the room. He didn't say anything, although Ben supposed he wouldn't if he thought he was alone. The wizard sighed, followed by the sound of cloth rustling. He sat quietly on the bed for a while after that.

"What do we do?" he mouthed at Zaara.

"We wait," she mouthed in return.

He sighed and thought he could hear Prima snickering in the background. Honestly, he didn't want her to have the satisfaction of watching him trapped out there.

Standing for too long was an issue and he gave up and considered how best to sit, but the sound of shrieking and several chimes issued from the direction of the throne room. Zaara's head jerked up, and in the room, Kural gave an exclamation of surprise—and worry.

Ben grabbed at her arm. "Whatever this is, it seems like he's not part of it," he said quietly.

She only gave him a doubtful look and pressed her ear against the door. More rustling was followed by footsteps, and a door slammed. She waited, eased the door open, and nodded to him.

"Okay, let's go see what's going on. Whether or not he's involved, it doesn't sound good."

CHAPTER TWENTY-TWO

This time, Zaara waited for Ben although she hurried him through the hallways. Wherever the fae tended to gather during the day, they now raced to the throne room. Once or twice, Ben caught a glimpse of Kural, also running, as well as Trin and the orc but he did not see Yn'solde anywhere.

That made sense, he thought sourly.

He still could not believe that she had somehow conspired to kill the king. It did not fit with anything he knew of her—which admittedly was very little. Why would someone who strove to be so apolitical conspire in an assassination?

And if she *were* an assassin, why would she have waited so many years?

No. There had to be another explanation and he intended to find it. Whatever was going on there had more layers than only this one, and he felt he was close to finding the truth.

Outside the throne room, he stopped Zaara. The fae had raced ahead and they were the only ones still there, so he could speak freely.

"Whatever happens," he told her, "it'll be all right."

The hopelessness in her eyes gutted him. "No," she said quietly, "it won't. Because if it *is* him, I'll have lost a mentor and a friend—and the only person I knew who could help me become what I'm meant to be. Being a wizard is a lonely business. I can't embark on that journey alone."

Ben smiled at that. "If I've learned anything from the past few days, it's that you can do anything you put your mind to. Better you do it alone than be guided by a murderer—and if I know you, in a hundred and fifty years, you'll be training someone new and using this as a reminder to stay true to yourself."

Her chin trembled. She wiped her eyes almost angrily.

"I didn't mean to make you cry," he said awkwardly. How did he always manage to mess these moments up?

He could see now that he hadn't always been there for Eve. Whatever her faults, he had also failed.

But he was trying to be better and he still made Zaara cry.

She laughed. "They aren't *bad* tears. I merely don't like crying. It's been...I lost someone. Recently. One of the bravest, kindest people I ever knew. I wish she was here so she could tell me what to do."

"You know what to do," he told her.

To his surprise, she hesitated, then reached around his neck. He froze. Did she plan to kiss him? He wasn't entirely sure he wanted that. It had been a strange few days. He was trying to sort through a tumble of emotions—she *was* undeniably good looking, but also this was a game and he wasn't interested in her and —when he realized she was tapping the sword he wore on his back.

"You know what to do too," she told him. "And that's to do the best you can to protect innocent people—including yourself. Promise me, before we go in there and before whatever happens next, that you'll do the best you can to make the world safer, however you need to do it."

"I'll…try." He couldn't lie to her.

She responded with a wry smile. "I'll try, too. Let's hope the world can get by on our best efforts."

"Well, when you put it that way, I think we might all be fucked."

Zaara was startled into a genuine laugh. She ushered him through the door and stifled the sound behind her hand so that people wouldn't notice them laughing during what was clearly a crisis.

"Wait." Ben looked up as he hobbled forward. "Zaara, where's the throne?"

Her head jerked up. "Oh, no. Where *is* the—no, I see it. It's on the floor." Her voice changed and became fearful. "I don't understand. Oh, gods, what if we're too late?"

His heart lurched and sank. He began to hobble faster, his mind a blank. If the king was dead, it didn't matter how fast he walked, but he could feel himself putting the effort in now that he should have put in days before.

If he'd been able to confront the assassins on the first night, if he'd been willing to stay and pry the truth out of Alia, if he'd insisted that Zaara come up with a plan when they first spoke about it, and if he'd warned the king, this moment might have been avoided.

He had left the choice of what was right in the hands of others and now, the king was dead and it was his fault. His chest felt like a storm roiled within when they broke through the crowd and he was so deep in his despair that he did not grasp what he saw.

When he'd first arrived, he had thought that the crystal of the structure was fashioned to look like grass, simply a good likeness of growing things. Now, he realized that the entire palace was, in fact, alive—right down to the dais and the king's throne.

Ben saw this clearly because it was dying. The dais had fallen in on itself, withered, and crumbled, and the death began to spread beneath their feet to consume the little seating areas and the lights.

In the center of what had once been the throne, the king stretched his hand out to grasp Kural's robes. He was feverish and weak, but he was alive, something Ben could hardly process. The monarch's eyes were bulging and over-bright over gaunt cheeks, and he whispered urgently.

Kural looked up, saw the others, and pure relief slid into his face. "Zaara. I need your help."

"No," the king rasped.

She froze and looked from her mentor to the king. Ben felt the tension vibrating through her. The fae watched her and whispered snidely. The guards held them back, but their obedience to that order *and* the guards' obedience to it seemed to be weakening. He could imagine the humans in the hands of an angry mob.

The king whispered something to Kural. The wizard grimaced but levered him upright.

With effort, the fae sovereign looked at all of them before he began to speak. "War…is coming."

A hastily indrawn breath reflected the collective shock and people began to whisper.

"The army approaches," he rasped. "They burn the land and attack the sacred wells. I have tried to maintain the health of the land, but I am drained."

"Because he's tied to it," Zaara whispered. She looked at Ben. "If they destroy the sacred wells, they kill *him*." Her gaze fixed on Kural and it looked as if she would cry.

"Go," the king told them all. "Prepare. They will be here soon. If they destroy the heart of the palace…they will destroy these lands."

He had thought the fae were flighty and childlike, but with their entire land in the balance, they moved with grim determination. The guards flew to the exits with their pikes held at the ready and some of the fae followed them with power crackling at their fingertips.

Ben could only be glad that they had settled on petty snubs instead of outright harm because he was fairly sure he would be dead in a pile of ashes if any of them had seriously tried to kill him.

About to breathe a sigh of relief, he froze and almost fell when Zaara left his side in a rush. A yell and a tumble of robes startled him and when it settled, she held her knife to Kural's neck. The wizard scrabbled at her hand and gasped questions, and she all but hissed something in his ear, her voice furious.

"Zaara!" Ben called.

"No," she replied and looked him in the eyes. "This has to end. He did this and he can undo it—I'll *make* him undo it if it's the last thing I do."

"Zaara." The wizard choked over the word. "I didn't—"

He looked around in horror. Trin stood frozen. He had weapons on him and was trained to use them. The man might have helped if there was any hope of getting to Kural before she finished the job.

There wasn't.

Beside the human, the orc watched the scene with narrowed eyes. He seemed more academically interested than anything. Where Trin was frozen with horror, the orc seemed to have accepted his helplessness and simply wanted to see how it would play out.

The king put a stop to it. "Put the knife down," he ordered. His voice was weak but he still had a shadow of his old authority. "Young wizard, you do not know what is truly happening."

Zaara froze. She met the monarch's gaze and whatever passed between them, she moved the knife away from Kural's neck. The wizard fell, gasping for air as he ran his fingers over the unbroken skin at the front of his throat. His disbelief was etched on his face.

"You…think he has done this." The king held himself half up with difficulty. "That he has killed me."

"He knew what would happen if the wells were destroyed," she whispered. "We found his notes."

Kural looked sharply at her, then at the king.

"Because I told him," the fae sovereign said simply. He collapsed onto the ruins of the throne and panted from his effort. "I have known for days that the army approached, and I enlisted the wizard's help to keep them back."

"What?" She looked at her mentor. "Why didn't you tell me?"

He hesitated before he said wryly, "Because two women were overheard in the palace, speaking about taking the king's life. One of the guards heard them on his rounds. He did not know which two women they were, and…" He shrugged

Zaara's eyes closed. "And you thought I might be one of them."

"I did not want to believe it," he told her, "but I could not take the chance."

"Wait." Ben looked from one to the other. "If it wasn't Zaara and it wasn't Kural…it *has* to be Alia and Yn'solde, doesn't it?"

"One would think so," the king said. He seemed to have found some humor in it. "For the record, I did not particularly suspect the wizard's apprentice. She…lacks subtlety."

Kural burst out laughing but swallowed his laughter in a cough when she looked sharply at him. He shrugged at her, unrepentant. "He's right, you know. If you planned to kill the king, you'd simply have done it. There wouldn't be any cloak and dagger games or an army marching through to destroy the sacred wells. You'd have done it all yourself."

Zaara threw her hands up.

"Okay, but if it's Alia and Yn'solde," Ben interjected, "where is Yn'solde? And why in hell would she do this?"

"We don't have time for why right now," the wizard said

bluntly. "We have to stop what she's set in motion. All we know is that the army is marching this way and Yn'solde is missing."

"Let me speak to Alia," Trin said suddenly. "If she did conspire —and I don't understand it, but it could only have been her— she'll know what Yn'solde planned. Maybe we can find a weakness in the plan. Maybe…" His voice trailed off. "What?"

The king looked at him with sorrow. "I am so sorry, child." He waved a hand and Kural bit his lip before he moved to a shrouded object in the corner. He hesitated, then pulled the shroud back to show Alia's still form.

Trin uttered a cry of sorrow. He ran to the woman's body and knelt at her side to touch her face and shake her as if there were any hope of waking her.

"She is not dead by my hand," the king said quietly. "We had called her to us to question her and a spell took her before we could do so. Whoever else is involved in this, they covered their tracks well. They made it impossible for her to speak the truth of what she was doing."

"When she told me it was her own business," Ben said slowly, "she was hiding it because she knew she couldn't tell me. She couldn't warn me." He looked at Kural. "Of course, she also said you knew the negotiations would fail."

"I know no such thing," Kural said stiffly.

The king laughed. "Peace, wizard. I know your thoughts on my kind."

"Then why trust him?" Zaara demanded.

"Because I could see the truth of his words," the monarch told her simply. "It is not magic, little one, only many years spent on this earth. The wizard does not like my kind, nor did he have great hopes for this peace treaty—but there was no malice there. When a life was in the balance, he was willing to work to save me."

She nodded mechanically. Wizard and apprentice looked at each other and Ben saw, with some relief, the same apology come to both their minds and then acknowledgment of it. They both smiled slightly and looked away.

A hollow boom echoed outside in the next moment, however, and everyone looked toward the front of the castle.

"The army is here," the king said quietly. "It is time, I think… to meet my enemy. I am curious as to her reasons for this."

CHAPTER TWENTY-THREE

Kural fashioned another floating litter much as he had done for Ben. He walked beside it as Zaara and Ben trailed behind. The orc, they noticed, stayed near Trin. He gave them a small nod as they left.

It was good that someone was there with him. Grief was complicated enough on its own, and there was much more to this death than simply bad luck. Whatever Trin and Alia had fled, they had done so together and they had taken shelter far from home with only each other for support. He believed the man truly had not known of her choices and now, he would never understand her reasons.

As they walked, however, his sadness was tempered by Zaara's relief.

"You were right," he said quietly.

"I—what?"

"You were right. Kural was no traitor."

She could not hide her smile. "Yes. It is…good. I knew what I had to do if he was a traitor, but I did not want to do it."

The wizard looked over his shoulder with a smile and she flushed. "If nothing else," the man called, "it takes a great deal of courage to confront a powerful wizard. Of course, you know what they say about courage."

Zaara's face said she knew this was a trap. "What do they say?" she asked finally.

"That there's a fine line between courage and stupidity," he replied. He chuckled at his joke and returned to speaking to the king.

She rolled her eyes and muttered.

"Just think," Ben told her, "you get to put up with this for… well, however long wizard training takes."

The woman groaned. "*Decades.*"

"Decades of dad jokes." He chucked. "You're screwed."

"You know, I don't think I could make it through this trying time without your support," she said acidly.

"Uh-huh."

They arrived at the front of the palace a few moments later. Fae appeared from all quarters, armed and with crystal armor. Word of Kural and Zaara's fight must have spread together with the king's judgment, as Ben noticed a different feel in the stares and whispers.

The fae no longer wanted to rip his eyes out. That was something good.

When he saw the army waiting outside the palace, he wished he'd set the bar a little higher for what constituted good news.

There were easily two thousand of them, probably more. It wasn't the elven army he had expected—like something out of a fantasy movie with identical green cloaks and blond hairdos. Instead, an imposing crew of humans, elves, dwarves, and orcs stood impassively, none of them wearing the same armor. They didn't stand in orderly rows either and looked like they might simply attack and destroy the palace.

The threat was visceral, and it was in their eyes and in the way they held their weapons. There was no law there and no honor. They brought only destruction, and they would observe none of the rules of the battlefield.

Ben scanned their ranks.

"Where's Yn'solde?" he whispered to Zaara.

Her face darkened. "Staying out of it," she whispered in return. "As usual. She doesn't want to get her hands dirty, after all."

He grimaced.

Ahead of them, the king and Kural exchanged a quiet few words before the wizard made a small gesture and touched the royal's shoulder. The king sat a little straighter and his voice, when he spoke, had the power Ben remembered from their first meeting.

"Who speaks for this army?"

"I do." An orc stepped forward. He was short by orcish standards and his skin had a bluish hue. There were no markings on his armor, nor did he wear a single piece of distinguishing jewelry. Ben scanned the other orcs present but saw none with blue skin and none without tattoos or jewelry.

"He's one of the water tribe," Zaara whispered when she noticed his scrutiny. "They were almost wiped out some years ago but he must have escaped. He doesn't have any tattoos or jewelry to claim tribe membership. It's...unusual for orcs."

He nodded.

The orc looked at the king, unimpressed, and simply waited.

"Who has sent you?" the fae sovereign asked finally. "Who has told you how to destroy the sacred wells?"

"It doesn't matter," the invader said carelessly. "We are here to end this—all of it. The wells must be destroyed. Either you let us do it quickly or we do it the hard way." His gaze traveled over the castle and the ranks of the assembled fae. "For your people's sake—"

"My people will not survive without the wells," the king said bluntly. "What you propose is death for all of them, not only for me."

The orc was silent for a moment. Was he thinking about his tribe? Ben could only wonder.

But if he hoped for mercy or kindness, he was disappointed.

"Quickly or slowly," he said again. "You choose." His eyes said that he wanted the king to let him draw this out.

"Where's Yn'solde?" Ben asked before he could stop himself.

The warrior looked curiously at him. "It's nothing to you. You're not fae."

"Neither are you," he retorted.

Zaara looked from one to the other, as did Kural, but neither seemed to want to stop this. Ben got the sense that they hoped to accomplish a spell if they had the time.

"I'm getting paid," the orc said. "There's the difference."

"You watched your tribe destroyed," he told him, taking a gamble, "and you'd do the same to someone else's on purpose?"

The warrior's eyes narrowed and a few of his comrades stepped back slightly. He had touched a nerve, one even they were afraid to prod.

Which in turn meant he was getting somewhere. Even if the orc was furious, the battle was being delayed.

"You dare speak of the water tribe?" the orc asked dangerously.

"It's a wonder *you* dare speak of them," Zaara said strongly from Ben's side. "They are rebuilding now and have called a meeting of all the tribes, and they do it without you—because you left them. There were those who kept them alive and those who defended them from the false god who would have destroyed them all. You merely came here to pay your anger forward to the whole world."

"You know nothing about me!" he snapped. "Have you watched your home destroyed? There are forces in this world bigger than one person, forces no one can stand against."

Ben, who had begun to be truly curious about what had happened to the water tribe, traded off with Zaara after a quiet nod from Kural.

"There *are* forces greater than any one person," he agreed, "but the force you speak of is a single elven woman."

"You think this is one woman?" the orc asked him. "That one person would order this and for no reason?"

"Then tell me the reason," he challenged. "If there's such a good reason—if there's an overwhelming force none of us can stand against—tell us what it is."

The warrior narrowed his eyes again. "Why?" he demanded.

"Because together, we might stand against it. Your army and all of the fae are more than a single person. Far more."

For a moment, sadness flickered on the orc's face before he said quietly, "There are worse things than death, human."

Ben stared at him. Something had changed and shifted, and he did not know what it was.

"Do you want to know why I left? Because I did not want to live a half-life. I left when they stopped singing their hymns and when they shushed babies in the cradle. Whatever cruelty you think I inflict on this kingdom, it is better they die now than live to see what is coming."

"That is not your choice to make," he said quietly. "You left. You chose for you—although one could also say you abandoned your people when they needed you most. Now you think you should be the one to decide which lives are worth living?"

"I know more than you do about what makes a life worth living."

He laughed wildly and thought of sun on his back and rock under his fingers, of snow blowing in his face, and his feet sure on the ground. "I wouldn't bet on that," he told him dangerously. "You don't know what I've seen and you don't know what I've lost. I'm here by the grace of those who wouldn't give up on me, and I'll be damned if I let you choose death for an entire race."

It was true, he realized in surprise. A week and a half earlier, he hadn't thought beyond the limits of the hospital bed. He had believed, in his darkest moments, that there was no point in trying to recover if he might not have everything he once had.

And somehow, this world—this make-believe world—had sent all that to the background. Even as he struggled to learn how to walk and use his hands and arms again, even though he lacked all the things he had thought made life worth living, he had found a purpose. He had found something larger than himself.

But the orc only shook his head. "Human, you know very little about what will be. You do not even know where the battle is occurring."

Ben did not know what to say to that but he didn't have time to think of an answer. The enemy leader raised his sword in a challenge and charged, and the army followed with a roar.

Zaara screamed something and Kural yelled in response. She hurdled the litter and sprinted toward the orc. Ben called her name, horrified, but she launched into combat with a grace he had not expected.

She wielded her single dagger lightning-fast and actual lightning seemed to spring from her other hand. Her adversary might have a sword, not to mention a serious height advantage, but she held her own.

Ben grasped the back of the litter as the king's guard formed a protective ring around them. He looked into the monarch's feverish eyes and saw his despair.

"What do you need?" he asked.

"I need to get…to the well. In the palace. I need…time…"

He swallowed. "I'll try to buy it for you."

And, his heart in his throat, he drew his sword.

CHAPTER TWENTY-FOUR

Ben expected that the fae line would shatter as soon as the mercenary army clashed with them. The fae might be armed, but he still had trouble seeing them as anything more than little elementals flitting around like Tinkerbell.

They turned out to be distressingly bloodthirsty.

Crystal staves flashed and plunged and were yanked back covered in multiple colors of blood. The line began to buckle once or twice but held.

He tightened his fingers around the haft of the sword. "We need to get back to the castle!" he yelled to Kural.

The wizard nodded tightly. The path to the castle, a broad causeway that tapered to the gate, was not exactly made for defense. They were already surrounded by the army, which had rushed forward to batter the door.

The well in the palace. There was a sacred well somewhere and the king needed to get to it—and unless Ben was very much mistaken, the army knew it was there.

What the hell had Yn'solde been playing at? If she knew all this, why not simply kill the king? Why not—

A battle-ax sliced through the line of fae guards. His entire body went rigid as blood spattered across his face, his lips, and even in his mouth. He gasped for air and stumbled back. Through a hole in the fae line, he could see the orc who swung the massive weapon.

The warrior was well over seven feet tall and didn't look winded from swinging a piece of metal almost the diameter of a hula hoop.

Hula hoop? Where was his head?

"Ben! Do something!"

Right. He swung the sword with all his might. It bit into the handle of the downed ax so hard that his palms went numb.

"What the hell were you aiming for?" Prima demanded.

"I thought I could cut it!" He wrenched the sword out, swung one leg up awkwardly, and brought it down on the handle of the ax.

"What are you doing?"

"Disarming him! Stop distracting me!" He hopped awkwardly on one leg and sprawled on the ground. "Fuck."

He hadn't managed to make the orc drop the weapon. With a growl and a bloodthirsty grin, it heaved it over its head and prepared to swing it down on him.

At the last minute, he rolled. It was the only thought in his head as the ax rose. His entire focus narrowed to the long, curved blade, so wickedly sharp, and the muscles in his torso twitched. Numb fingers clutched uselessly at the sword. The blade was dented and it would only hinder him, but he couldn't seem to let it go.

He had to roll. *Wait. Wait. Wait.* Everything came down to this. He could do it.

While he had focused on the orc, though, his adversary had focused on him. As soon as his arms rose, two of the fae guards darted in with their wicked blades and found the gaps in the shoulders of the enemy's makeshift armor. Deep-green blood spurted, and the warrior dropped the weapon behind him.

From the scream, he must have killed or injured one of his own with the weapon, but Ben didn't have any time to think about it. He scrambled up, fell again, and caught himself on the litter.

He could do this. All he had to do was move again. It didn't matter that he couldn't move *well*, only that he had to get through this.

Ben had never considered how loud a battle would be or how close death would be. There was still blood on his face, and the orc drew his last gasps nearby as crystal pikes were thrust repeatedly into his flesh.

A shout caught his attention. An elf attacked the new gap in the line. This one was different from Yn'solde in almost every way he could imagine, from the half-shaved head to the orcish tattoos, but one thing was the same. He moved with perfect grace.

Without taking time to think, he pushed away from the litter and snatched the hilt of his sword in both hands. He swept it at an angle and knocked the enemy's blade aside.

Into himself, of course, and he fell in a heap. But between the unexpected block and the fact that he threw a leg up, the elf also sprawled in the dirt.

"End him!" Kural yelled. "We need to start the retreat. They're opening the path for us!"

He pushed to his knees, his hands on the sword as the elf rolled and stood. The areas of weakness jumped out at him with painful clarity—the Achilles tendon, the femoral artery, and the gap between the stomach and the breastplate. He could do it and it didn't require any particular grace. All he had to do was swing the sword with all his might and pull across the skin.

Everything seemed to freeze. He couldn't do it.

"Ben!"

"Ben!"

The voices penetrated and he shook his head violently and

fought down the roiling nausea. The elf readied himself for a strike to push through to the king.

Ben's shoulder met the side of his thigh. He'd never played football but he'd seen enough of it to know to tackle that way. His momentum carried the assailant over at the same time that lightning caught the elf in the face. He sprawled and dragged in a breath before he scrambled up the elf's body to try to pin his arms. His foe's face was blackened and burned.

There was no life in his eyes.

"Ben!" Kural caught hold of his arm in a vice-like grip. "Come *on!*"

They stumbled across the bridge with the army pressed around them.

"Where's Zaara?" he asked.

"Doing a hell of a lot better than *you,*" the wizard snapped. "You can't count on having one of us to guard you every time! Can you do this or not?"

He felt a flush of anger mixed with shame. "I didn't ask for any of this," he muttered, as much to himself as to anyone else.

Still, he knew it didn't matter. He might not have asked for it but it was happening. And when the body of one of the fae guards fluttered to land beside him, he knew, with a sinking feeling, that this army didn't give a damn whether or not he wanted to hurt them.

They pushed forward and he blocked and parried for all he was worth. More than once, a blade missed him by inches and a few times, a shield or a fist or a blade struck him. He couldn't even bring himself to yell the first time it happened. He stared at the blood welling from his arm in shock and tried to remember how to move his feet.

"Ben!" Zaara called urgently. "Your arms and legs can get injured. Protect your body! *Kural!*"

"I have other priorities right now!" the wizard roared.

She was still trying to defeat the head of the mercenary army and was bleeding as well. A long gash ran from the top of her forehead and through her eyebrow. Blood coated one cheek, but she fought with barely a wince.

The clanless orc had suffered injuries too, but he wielded his weapons with an ease she didn't have. While she might not abhor violence when it came to defense, she didn't want to hurt anyone unnecessarily. She didn't relish the feeling of defeating an enemy, much less killing them.

The enemy, on the other hand, certainly did.

Fury rose in Ben's chest. He threw himself between the litter and an attacking human soldier. Although he didn't have the coordination for most blows, he had enough to bring his knee up with a good degree of force. The soldier doubled over and he shoulder-checked him off the edge of the causeway.

A spurt of blood told him that the fall had not been painless, and he felt as though ice water had been poured over him. He was doing the best he could, goddammit, but he still didn't want to kill anyone.

A shout came from behind him. The guards had cleared a path to the door and were opening it enough to let the king's litter through.

"Zaara!" Ben yelled.

She cast one desperate look over her shoulder and the orc seized his chance. He thrust with all his might and Ben screamed at the top of his lungs.

The woman whipped around and one hip turned sideways. The sword snagged on the front of her leather armor as the blade slid past her. From her gasp of pain, he could tell that the blade had touched her skin, but it hadn't done nearly the damage the orc had hoped.

More than that, she still had her dagger. Time seemed to slow around him and Kural dragged him back as Zaara planted her front foot and drove the dagger through the orc's eye.

The massive warrior thudded to his knees and she didn't wait for him to die. She wrenched the blade free and ran toward the defenders with one hand pressed over her stomach to stem the blood that seeped through her fingers. She ran without looking back as the mercenaries saw their leader fall and raced after her.

The doors began to swing shut and Ben yelled for them to stop. He threw himself against one of them to slow it, but he couldn't hold them forever.

When one of the mercenaries caught the back of Zaara's shirt, he knew she wouldn't make it.

For the life of him, he couldn't understand why he did what he did next. He launched himself out of the doorway, skidded along the causeway—flailing wildly to keep his balance—and grasped the human who tried to catch Zaara. When he pounded the hilt of his sword on the man's head and kicked him, his fingers loosened.

"Go!" Ben called to Zaara.

She wouldn't leave him. Her blood-slick hand extended to grasp his and she dragged him into the palace a second before the doors slammed shut.

He collapsed, heaving desperate breaths. "Zaara—are you—"

"It looks worse than it is." She was panting and her voice was tight, but she stayed upright. "You?"

"I, uh—" He went to take an inventory of his wounds and decided against it. "A lot of me hurts but I don't seem to be bleeding out. So I have that going for me."

"Also, you managed to stop being totally useless," Prima interjected.

"Shut up," he muttered.

"No one is suggesting you turn into a mass-murderer, you know."

"I said, shut up!"

"Um, Ben?" Zaara frowned at him in concern. "Who are you talking to?

"No one. It's not important. I swear I'm not bleeding out."

"Okay, that's good enough." She looked doubtful but chose

not to waste time on it and simply leaned forward to help him up. The two of them followed the litter that now moved toward the doors at the opposite side of the throne room.

The entrance doors shuddered behind them as the mercenaries threw themselves at them and battered the barrier with axes and swords. Ben looked over his shoulder once or twice, but there was nothing to be done. The battle was raging outside. All they could do was catch the stragglers.

It was a surprisingly vulnerable feeling.

"Where's the well?" he asked Zaara.

"It's—oh, *fuck.*"

With a crack and the sound of shattering glass, a section of one wall fell to pieces. Fae and mercenaries alike poured through the gap and swept around to reach the king.

"*Run!*" Zaara yelled.

She and Ben sprinted with every ounce of strength they could muster. He was aware that his legs were getting tangled and his arms flailed wildly, but there was nothing he could do about it. Kural and the guards ran alongside the litter and tried to get to the next set of doors. Arrows whistled and were followed by the screams from humans, elves, and fae.

The small party around the king thrust forward into the darkness and through the doors that opened and closed with magical force, but they weren't alone. Mercenaries had pushed in with them, which led to a pitched and desperate battle around the king's litter.

In the darkness, the well glowed a pale blue, unsettlingly beautiful.

And on the far side of it, a shadow waited.

Ben's breath caught. The mercenary leader had said they didn't know who they were fighting or where they should be. He had told them although it hadn't made sense.

Yn'solde had come to finish the job herself.

CHAPTER TWENTY-FIVE

Battles raged on either side of the closed doors. Kural swung his staff with abandon, as much for magic as to thwack mercenary heads, and Zaara had thrown herself into the fray without a word of complaint. They held the mercenaries at bay for now and it looked like they might still triumph, but Ben didn't know how much time they had.

There was no one else. He had to stop this.

His heart thudded as he walked to the edge of the pool and met Yn'solde's gaze. She looked different now. Her hair was pulled back severely and she was dressed in clothes that were made for travel and fighting. In the light filtering from the well, she looked haunted.

"I don't understand why," he said bluntly.

That surprised her. She had watched him with a sardonic expression and now, she stared at him.

"I told you why," she said after a moment. "He's *always* gotten what he wanted."

"And he wants to destroy the fae," he said.

"No." She seemed impatient now and looked at the shimmering blue. "He wants *this*—this power. He wants it at his beck and call. I held him off for a time, but now…there's nothing left for it."

The pieces began to fall into place in his head with sickening clarity.

"You were sent here to kill the king," he said. "You never fled of your own volition."

"I volunteered." She looked at him. "I didn't want to do it, though. I was desperate to get out."

"Like that makes a difference," Ben said. His heart pounded and he could barely hear anything over the thumping in his ears.

Unexpectedly, he had touched a sore point. She drew herself tall and her lip curled. "It made a difference," she told him, her voice low. "I held my brother off for *years*. I found out the king was linked to the sacred wells and told him that killing the king wouldn't give him everything he wanted. Anyone else he sent would simply have done it, no questions asked."

"That makes you far from blameless," he retorted. "Do you honestly think that wipes away the blood on your hands?"

"Are you honestly so stupid that you couldn't see this was inevitable?" Her voice rose now.

"How was it inevitable?" Ben waved his hands dismissively. "You said he always gets what he wants. Didn't you ever think that *maybe* it was because people keep doing his dirty work for him? People like you?"

"You have *no idea* what it's like!" Her hair escaped its braid here and there. "He tortured our brother to death, he had our sister and our mother killed, he killed his wife, and he has hundreds who will do his bidding if he raises a single finger. There was never a chance to stand up to him."

"Coward," he said simply. "You could have ended it."

"How?"

"You could have killed *him*! You spent years here, ingratiating yourself with the king and the court and learning their foibles. If you had done that to your brother, you could have defeated him and won the loyalty of his friends and his guards. But you played by *his* rules and now, here we are." He shook his head. "And I don't even get it. You're murdering an entire race, destroying a species, and for what?"

"So he won't get it!" She practically screamed the words at him. "I can't keep him from sinking his claws into this land, but I can damned well keep him from getting his hands on the magic. And if that's all I can do, then I'll do it!"

Ben closed his eyes.

"Hate me all you want." Strength had returned to her voice. "Think whatever you want, but I'll know that in the end, I kept him from getting stronger."

"No. In the end, you missed your chance to bring him to justice." He spoke the words with a cutting edge of disgust. She began to circle toward him and he inched away, trying to keep his distance.

She absolutely could *not* find out how useless he was with this sword.

"You told me who you were the second day we were here," he said bitterly to her. "You said to stay out of the fights and not attract attention. That's what you did with your brother, wasn't it? You never tried to start a rebellion or to stand up to him. You came here because it gave you the chance to escape and now, you're making the entire fae race pay for your grudge against him."

"Grudge? If he pollutes the wells, he has them all in the palm of his hand! Don't you understand? He'll be able to use them as slaves and will have an unstoppable army."

"And you could have kept it from coming to this." He only narrowly avoided pounding the tip of his sword against the ground for emphasis. That seemed like the wrong thing to do with a sharp object and a stone floor. "He put your back to the wall but you're the one who dragged other people in with you."

Genuine hatred flared in her eyes. "You know nothing about me," she said quietly, but he heard her voice tremble.

His heart sank because he hadn't wanted to be right about this. He had wanted her to tell him something—anything—that would help him to understand.

But there wasn't anything she could say to explain it all away. She had been dealt a hard hand but she had chosen her path, and it was one that would doom hundreds of thousands. Selfishly, she hadn't asked the fae what they thought and hadn't enlisted them.

Instead, she had told the mercenaries how to destroy the wells.

Yn'solde looked at the king and moved her hand to a pouch at her belt. Ben didn't need any prompting to know it contained poison. He also knew what it would do when she threw it in the well.

"What about Alia?" He asked the question desperately in an attempt to distract her.

She gave him a curious look. "Alia?"

"The woman you got to help you?"

"What about her?" She looked blankly at him.

"She's *dead*."

"We'll all be dead soon," she told him. "The mercenaries will leave no one alive except me, and my brother will kill me once he finds out what I've done."

Ben wanted to scream but he bit it back. "You're exactly like him."

"I am *nothing* like him."

"You're sacrificing people for your goal and you don't even grieve them." He stopped counter-circling and began to walk toward her. "No more."

"No more? It's done." She drew a short sword from its sheath and faced him. "Nothing you can do will stem the tide now, human."

"You will still come to justice," he told her.

Her gaze traveled over him. "You did so well to convince us that you were injured. I only began to doubt when I saw you reach the throne room the other day and even then, I wouldn't have guessed you could wield a sword."

He merely smiled. His heart beat wildly and he tried to school his features to hide it.

What in God's name was his plan here? He tried to delay the fight because there was no way he could win it but sooner or later, he would have to throw himself into the fray.

And if he intended to bring her to justice, that meant killing her. She wouldn't let herself be taken alive. He could believe that she'd slept with a knife beside her bed for years to make sure she could end her life before she was ever taken back to her brother.

Yn'solde was a woman who was trained to be an assassin, who had no morals, and had no hope of surviving this.

His odds were *not* good. Why hadn't he thought to play his weakness up? Then, at least, she might have underestimated him.

She drove forward in a charge. He could see in her eyes that she was testing him. She held one arm back for balance and wielded the short-sword effortlessly with her front hand.

Ben batted her sword away with his blade. It wasn't a graceful movement, but it worked. Her eyes narrowed and she circled so his back was to the water.

"You're injured," she told him.

"I'm aware." He raised an eyebrow. "Oh, that reminds me— your water orc friend is dead."

She gave a sharp look at the knot of fighters near the door and he took the opportunity to lunge forward. His sword barely nicked her before she danced back, but he felt it strike and bile rose in his throat. He thought of the soldier he had pushed off the causeway and the crystal blades of grass he must have landed on.

It occurred to him that he would throw up everywhere. He wondered if he could do so in her face, which might at least give him a tactical advantage.

"Hold it together," Prima told him. *"She's dangerous."*

The fact that she didn't mock him made him take notice. "I hate this," he murmured under his breath.

"Hate it all you want but stay alive."

Yn'solde's eyes narrowed at him as if sensing that something was going on beyond his façade, but with her blood spilled, she was more careful now.

Ben feinted left and moved right and almost caught her again. She ducked out of the way with a grimace and instead of moving back, he pressed the advantage. He wasn't sure what he was doing and only knew he wanted to keep her off-balance. They were testing one another but he had to end this soon.

Out of the corner of his eye, he saw Kural sneaking around the back of the room with the litter.

The wizard was trying to get to the well. Ben knew that immediately.

He made his decision equally quickly and followed his advance with a swing that his adversary could almost certainly evade. She did, but it turned her so her back was to the pool. He drove forward and then began a retreat.

The combat used everything he had and he was running out of energy. Every muscle ached. He barely kept his feet each time he shifted his weight and half his swings didn't seem to go where he intended them to—with the benefit, at least, that Yn'solde also had trouble predicting where he would strike next.

Pretending to falter, he let her drive him back. No matter what, he had to keep her distracted so she wouldn't notice that the king was close to the well. All their hopes rested on that. Whatever power the fae monarch might have, he had to be able to tap the well before she poisoned it.

"Answer me something," Ben said. He'd always been something of an asshole and he decided that if ever there was a time to use it, the time was now. "How the hell did you sit back and put up with him having killed your sister and your mother? Oh—and your brother."

Her mouth compressed into a thin line. "You can do an awful lot when there's no other choice."

"You had a choice," he said. "You chose to do what he wanted and fell into line. Your choice was to obey. You took the warning *exactly* like he meant you to."

"You don't know a thing about it!" She lost her temper then and advanced in a rush. Surprisingly, she was crying. "You do what you have to do to survive. You don't understand it—any of it. Don't you dare judge me."

"I'm judging you," he retorted harshly, "for what you're doing *now*. If you hadn't called in an army and tried to assassinate the king, maybe it would be a different story."

Behind her, the monarch had reached the water and Kural helped him to touch the surface.

Ben put his sword up to block her latest swing and stepped in close. "Send the army away," he said to her. "Call them off."

"Don't you see? I *can't*."

"Yes, you can. You can defy him and bolster his enemies, not simply scorch the earth to spite him." His mouth tasted like ashes.

"You have no idea how powerful he is." She shook her head.

"Maybe not," he said. "But I know which side I'm on."

He had no idea what tipped her off but she looked over her shoulder. Her shout of despair was one he would never forget, but what was worse was the grim determination with which she reached for the pouch at her belt. She dipped her fingers into it, ready to throw the powder.

There wasn't a choice, not anymore. It was her or however many *thousands* of fae. He looped his foot around hers, tripped her, and brought his sword down in her back. The life left her body with a powerful jerk that he felt, and he rolled away and heaved his guts out on the stone floor.

CHAPTER TWENTY-SIX

"**B**en!"

Feet pounded across the floor and in the next moment, Zaara was at his side. He shook her hands off as the touch made the nausea worse. When the spreading pool of blood touched his hand, he recoiled with an oath.

"Ben?" Bloodied and bruised, she crouched in front of him. "Please tell me you're okay." Her hands patted his arms and torso in search of wounds.

"I'm not…she didn't—" He hung his head.

"You gave her a chance," she said. Her words seemed to come from very far away. She bit her lip. "Ben, I think I did you a disservice when I first told you that you might have to kill people. I made it seem simpler than it was. I—"

"You're hurt." He couldn't listen to this right now, not with Yn'solde's body lying beside him. "We should get you help."

"It's not bad. I made sure there was no infection." She managed a shadow of a smile. "And, Ben, if you doubt yourself—"

"Don't."

"No, I mean it." She raised her finger and pointed behind him. "Look."

195

He turned his head curiously and drew in a sharp, startled breath.

The fae king hovered over the sacred well. His head was tipped toward the darkness of the cave's ceiling. Ben suddenly wondered how high the ceiling was or if there was one at all. Looking up gave him a strange sense of vertigo as if he stood at the edge of a void.

Blue light swirled up and around the king's thin form. He was still sick but he had begun to gain strength.

Ben looked over his shoulder to the throne room. He could still hear the clash of weapons and the shouts of soldiers on both sides. He let Zaara help him up and they looked from the closed doors to the king at the well.

Even Kural hung back. Ben had disliked the man for many reasons since he met him but something in his manner now made him more human than he'd ever expected. The wizard did not watch the power with hunger or envy but like a man who had heard a beautiful piece of music. He was a wizard because he loved magic, not because he coveted it, and he leaned heavily on his staff and simply watched. There was blood on his robes and he did not put equal weight on his left leg.

Beside him, Zaara watched with awe.

"What do you see?" he asked her. "What does it look like to an apprentice wizard?"

"Oh, this is beyond me." She didn't look at him. He didn't think there was anything in the world that could make her tear her gaze away. "I don't think I'd even call it a spell—or magic. Ben, it's like…staring at the smallest part of a pattern, a beautiful pattern, and knowing you could never *see* all of it and your mind couldn't hold it all."

He looked around. Was it only him or was the glow getting brighter?

"He's so old," she said, "and I think he must carry the memories of the others. The kings who went before. Or…"

"Or?" He looked curiously at her.

She met his gaze, her left eye swollen shut and half her face covered in dried blood. "Or they're still alive," she told him. "*In him, somehow—or in the spell. I don't think I can explain it.*"

Ben nodded and looked down. There were no words for how small this made him feel.

How useless, too.

"You stopped her," Zaara told him. She continued to watch him. "What's happening now…maybe it's beyond you or me, Ben, but we helped it to happen."

He looked at her. "I'm only one person. I killed…one soldier. And Yn'solde." Bile rose in his throat again. "And there are thousands out there."

They both looked again, toward the battle they were powerless to stop.

"You protected the king," she said. "And you defeated the one who would have doomed all of this." She shook her head. "To think she was in league with her brother the whole time. It was quite an act."

"Yes and no." His mouth twisted. "He wanted the sacred wells. She intended to destroy them to keep him from getting them."

"No." Her whispered protest sounded appalled.

"Yes." He looked sharply at her. "Do you think—should I not have—"

"Couldn't she have *told* the fae king?" Zaara exploded. "She hated her brother and she couldn't simply…fight him? She had to kill the fae and their lands to keep her brother from—ohhhh." She looked furiously at the body. "I knew I hated that man, but she's almost as bad. Hell, she might be worse."

Ben heaved a sigh of relief.

"And you weren't sure she deserved to die?" she asked skeptically a moment later.

"Well…"

"*She has a point,*" Prima interjected.

"You need to think about what you consider justice," Zaara said emphatically.

"I know I don't like being the sole arbiter of it." He looked away from the body on the floor. "And I know if it had been only me and not you and Kural, many more people would be dead. I'd have failed. So maybe it doesn't matter what I think."

"It doesn't seem like there's much point in speculating about that," she said thoughtfully after a moment.

A thud and a cracking sound from behind them startled them both. He backed away from the door and raised his sword and she readied her knife. She trembled with exhaustion, as did he, but there was no thought of laying their weapons down. There was only acceptance.

In the next moment, the well erupted. Ben sprawled onto the floor. His chin struck the rock so hard his teeth clacked together. He yelled and pushed up but froze to stare open-mouthed at the column of blue flame that streaked into the sky. There must, indeed, be no roof to this cavern, as he could see it ascend beyond the limit of his vision.

There was markedly less clanging and screaming outside the door now, although shouts that sounded like questions could be heard.

He squinted into the flame but could not see the king at all. His chin trembled when he allowed his mind to silently voice his suspicions. If someone had asked him to step into a column of flame and sacrifice himself, would he have had the courage to do it?

The magical blaze narrowed and began to pale. Columns spiraled up the sides of it.

"Zaara," he called. "I think it'll blow again!"

"Then put your head down, you moron!"

"Right!"

With a sound like a foghorn, the enchantment burst downward and out. It swept across his skin and he could swear he felt both the tearing force of hurricane winds and rain and nothing at all. The magic existed on another plane.

Out in the hall, there were cries of amazement but only the sound of fae voices. When the doors swung open of their own accord, he raised his head and saw that the mercenary soldiers had vanished.

"Gone." Zaara dragged in a breath. She scrambled to her feet. "They're all *gone.*"

As one, she and Ben turned to the well.

The figure who floated there was both the same and diminished. Kural hurried forward to help the fae king leave the well and the two exchanged quiet words. When the monarch went to the remaining guards, they fluttered around him and he reassured them softly.

He stopped at each fallen body and laid a hand on the brow of each guard. Ben's throat tightened. The king did not shy away from seeing those who had shielded his life with their own.

When he reached them, the young man swallowed hard.

"I am told it was you who felled the leader of the mercenary army," the fae sovereign said to Zaara.

"I—oh. Yes. Your Majesty." She bobbed her head in an awkward bow.

He touched her face and healing spread from his fingertips. Ben watched in amazement as the swelling subsided and the wound knit itself together. A scar remained, new and red, but she did not seem to mind it and smiled at the king in thanks.

"And you," the king said to him. "You also rose to the challenge, did you not?"

"I...Your Majesty..."

"You are not of this world," the monarch said. "I see no memories in you of our cities or our history. And still, you took up arms to defend my people."

"I..." *Killed.* But the royal's hand touched him as well, and even as the aches and pains eased in his body, he felt peace settle over him like a blanket.

The king looked at him for only a moment before he moved on to Yn'solde's body.

"Rest, young one," he told her. "When next your spirit rises, may you find peace."

He left the room and the others followed, Ben with a last glance at the elf's still form.

The room beyond held only the fae—the living and the dead. The living joined the king's procession and the humans fell ever farther back. Trin and the orc joined the swelling ranks of the king's followers.

It was outside the gates that the greatest change had been wrought. It looked as if there had never been a war at all. The trail of destruction behind the army had been wiped away. The blood was gone, as were the soldiers.

"Where's the army?" he whispered to Zaara. He wasn't sure he wanted to know the answer.

Kural was the one who answered. "Beyond the borders of fae and barred from returning."

"Ah." That was less gruesome than it might be. He nodded.

The king surveyed the land for some time before he turned to the assembled crowd.

"There is much to do." It was easy to see how much the magic had drained him, but he floated unbowed and strong.

Restored, he thought, and his heart lightened a little more.

CHAPTER TWENTY-SEVEN

Ben spent most of the next few days alone in his room.

Zaara and Kural were closeted with the king and some of the other leaders of the fae, trying to devise a peace treaty between them and Insea, which meant their company was limited. Trin had withdrawn into his chambers to conduct funeral rites for Alia, and the orc had apparently set out for his home to bring word of the fae to his tribe.

Ben set himself to practicing the exercises Zaara set him, and although he made impressive progress, he was also bored out of his mind. Walking had once been a completely absorbing task, as had almost anything. Now he could walk, pick himself up, wield a sword without threatening to decapitate himself, and do things like eat without flinging food over his shoulder.

Which meant he had time to dwell on how bored he was.

Kural found him on the ramparts on the third day. Where Zaara seemed more and more exhausted by the day, the wizard looked much the same as he always did. He would have guessed the man to be anywhere between his mid-thirties and mid-forties and still found it impressive how the mild-mannered man managed to look so young while being centuries old and vastly powerful.

Also, the blue had begun to fade nicely. He now merely looked like he might have a case of frostbite.

"Where will you go next?" Kural asked without preamble.

Ben looked sharply at him. "I—oh."

"Oh?" The wizard raised an eyebrow.

"I thought I would come with you." Now that he said it, he felt ridiculous. "That was stupid of me."

"You're welcome to travel with us, certainly." He nodded. "It would be cruel to leave someone with no money and no connections stranded in fae territory."

"So they haven't done an about-face and decided they like humans?"

Kural snorted. "That won't ever happen, boy. The king may have a good head on his shoulders, but the fae don't respect the other races worth a damn. I imagine it's hard to do when you're smarter than everyone else, but…" He forced a smile. "It doesn't help that they look like children to us."

"That does make it confusing," he agreed. He leaned on the parapet. "If I could maybe…accompany you out of these lands, that would be good."

"Of course." The man nodded. "Zaara assumed you would but I wanted to make sure. For all I knew, you'd want to stay here."

He shuddered dramatically. "I can't get out of this place fast enough. I never thought I'd say that about a beautiful castle with free food, but…"

There were so many horrifying memories from this place. In the throne room, he could see the withered throne and Alia's body. On the causeway, he could see the spurt of blood from the soldier he had pushed off. The palace would forever be the place that made him do things he could not reconcile with the man he was.

He looked away.

"I have to say," Kural said after a moment, "I've never seen someone as committed as you are to not killing. Most of us simply become accustomed to it."

Ben looked at the fields and the waving grasses. "You don't have to tell me that I cost lives. I know I did."

The wizard frowned at him in surprise. "That wasn't what I was going to say."

"Maybe it should have been." He pushed up and took a deep breath. "I thought avoiding violence was a philosophy that hinged first on my actions. But there were people who were a huge danger and stopping them could have prevented so much death." He looked at his companion. "I won't make the same mistake again."

The look the man gave him was, surprisingly, not so much disbelieving as pitying. "No," he said. "You'll make different ones. I don't say that to be cruel, Ben. I say it because you should know how life is. The older I get, the more I believe that we do the best we can, and we will never know if we did the right thing. The good we do is not defined by rigid rules, it is not defined by our effort or hardship, and it is not defined by our intentions."

A silence settled between them.

Kural's fingers tightened around his staff. "And I confess, I don't know what to do with that."

He left without another word and Ben looked after him.

"Is that what you think?" he asked Prima when he was alone.

"What do you mean?"

"Kural is you, isn't he? You made him. So, what he said—do you think it's true?"

"What a strange question," she said slowly. "Kural lives in some of my processes, yes. But he is not me and I am not him—or as much as I am him, I am also Zaara and the fae king and the palace. The part of me that is Kural says those things and believes them, exactly as other parts of me say and believe other things."

Ben considered this. "Isn't it confusing to believe more than one thing at a time?"

"I was under the impression that every human did."

"I…" He closed his mouth. "Actually, that's correct. We call it cognitive dissonance. Son of a bitch, I never thought about it that way."

"I merely have rather more bandwidth to do so."

"I don't envy you that," he said with a laugh.

"By the way, Zaara is looking for you."

"Oh, now you tell me these things?"

"I make exceptions sometimes."

He smiled as he walked quickly down the stairs and into the palace. While he'd made excellent progress, he wasn't close to his old level of coordination and certainly wouldn't trust his body to take him up a rockface safely. He could, however, walk without using all his concentration.

Zaara waved when she saw him approach. Her hair was held back in an ornate braid and she wore the fancy robes again. Against her finery, the scar over one side of her face was all the more noticeable.

The hat that went with it was still ridiculous.

"I'm glad I found you," she said. "The treaty is signed. We'll leave tomorrow."

"So soon?" Ben couldn't disguise his leap of happiness but he was also surprised. "I thought there'd be more…pomp and circumstance."

Great, now he had the graduation song stuck in his head.

"Usually, maybe." She looked evasive. "There's so much for everyone to do. The fae need to rebuild, and we need to get home."

"Ah, yes. The mysterious nature of—"

"*Not* here." Her tone was firm but she smiled. "Go and pack. There will be a feast tonight and we'll leave at dawn."

"So don't go hard at the feast?"

"Or if you do, try to pass out in the litter with your luggage packed." She smiled and headed to her room.

There was nothing for him to pack so he passed the time with a few more swordsmanship exercises. When he got to the feast, he was both ravenous and exhausted. He found his mind drifting as the night went on, and he turned in early without a goodbye to the king.

He couldn't face those eyes right now—eyes that saw far too much and far too clearly.

Then, he dreamed of the accident.

It was hot in the sunshine and the skin along his side itched when he stretched to the limit and sweat ran across an almost-burn. Grains of sand and stone were rough under his fingertips and the pressure on the ball of his left foot as he braced himself was vivid.

Now, however, he could feel what he hadn't felt that day. His body had tried to tell him something was wrong and in the dream, he could see himself ignoring it. There was a faint hitch in the muscles of his shoulders and his foot didn't grip the hold correctly.

Ben could remember, at last, what went on in his head as he felt for those holds. His mind was busy being angry about Mike and Eve, angry that they were challenging him about his job situation, while he tried to ignore the fact that he was tired of never having a home of his own.

His foot slipped.

He sat, drenched in sweat. There was only silence and pale light and the sound of his breathing.

A knock startled him and the door opened and Zaara stuck her head in.

"You're up already!" She looked pleased. "That'll help with—what's wrong?"

"It's nothing." Ben ran a hand through his hair and tried to breathe. "Tell me there's time for a shower."

"Shower?"

"Bath."

"Oh. Um, if you're quick. I can grab your bags." She took two of them and headed out.

He startled when a steaming bath and a cool one both blinked out of nowhere. He scrubbed quickly and dunked his head into the cold water to clear it.

"Was it a bad dream?" Prima asked.

He was about to snap that it sure hadn't been a good one, but he held his tongue and simply nodded. It was something else he was learning to do

How could he ever apologize to Mike? He closed his eyes for a moment.

"Prima? Can you tell them...I want to wake up? I mean...I want to come back, but..."

"I'll come up with something," she said. *"You won't blink out without warning. I'll bring you out tonight at the latest."*

"Thanks." He needed to talk to Mike before he lost his nerve.

He dressed in his magically cleaned clothes and hurried through the palace to the gates. Despite the beauty he knew was around him, he tried not to look because he didn't want to see it or remember it. It was beautiful and perhaps someday, he could return.

Maybe he would never be ready to do that, however. This wasn't a place for him, and it occurred to him that it might have been designed that way. It had been somewhere he wouldn't want to rest on his laurels for too long.

That thought made him smile.

He stepped out to find Zaara and Kural in a floating litter, their horses waiting alongside. He climbed in and looked around for propulsion systems.

"With so much magic in this land, the king thought it would make sense to give our horses a rest," the wizard explained. "We can rest and talk, at least until we're out of the fae lands—although Zaara may be sick of my voice by now."

She gave him a small smile. "I should hope I wouldn't get sick of you so fast—or vice versa. My training will last decades, remember."

"And I'm sure you'll keep me on my toes the whole time." Kural yawned and snapped his fingers, and a steaming teapot appeared in midair. "Who wants something to drink?"

"Tea?" Ben asked.

"Tea, coffee, chocolate—it's whatever you want." He smiled. "The elves have been a particular thorn in our side lately, but some of their spells are quite nice."

He took a cup gratefully. It turned out to be hot chocolate, as rich and thick as melted chocolate without being too cloying. With a happy sigh, he leaned forward to look at the platter of breads, cheeses, and fruit that Kural had made appear as well.

Then, while they were distracted and had their guard down, he asked calmly, "So, what's going on in Insea that peace is so vital?"

His companions both choked on their tea. He merely sipped his chocolate and smiled.

Zaara looked at the wizard. "I fucked up," she admitted baldly.

"It had to be you," her mentor pointed out.

"Yes, but I wanted to take responsibility."

"Noted. Don't go into politics." Kural looked at Ben. "I'm afraid this set of secrets is not common knowledge for a reason. Suffice it to say we have it on good authority that the world will become a great deal more violent and prone to war if no action is taken. For this reason, we are seeking to pre-emptively bind the various nations into cooperation with one another. Mutually beneficial trade seems to be one of the best ways to do so."

She nodded and added, "There are things like the new elven 'king.' You know conflicts will come out of that, so you should plan ahead."

"Hmm." Ben leaned back and munched on a bagel-like object that seemed to have the cream cheese already inside it. The concept was intriguing and it was delicious.

"We should talk about where you'll go after this," Zaara told him. "We'll travel back to Insea and you're welcome to come with us. If nothing else, you should be able to find employment there. We might also be able to introduce you to Justin—that is if he's not back to arguing with the human leaders."

Kural gave a despairing snort. "If it's possible to have a worse job than the one we did, he has it. Did you see his latest letter?" His eyes lit up with conspiratorial glee as he looked at her. "Lord Gyforde tried to trap *both* of them into marriage with his daughter."

"Well, that's merely a rite of passage in the human political world," she quipped. She looked at Ben. "He does it with everyone. *Everyone.* Also, and this is important, she's four. He started doing this before he even had a daughter." She looked at the sky. "Maybe I'll help her run away when she's old enough."

"You should," Kural said with unexpected vehemence.

"Ben?" Prima spoke quietly. *"Tell them you want to take a nap."*

Ben yawned. "Oh, man. I'm still tired. Would you mind if I took a nap?"

"Not at all." Kural gestured to the expanse of pillows. "And you might sleep a good while longer than you anticipate. These fields are filled with all manner of sleep spells. It won't do you any harm. If anything, it would do you good." He yawned as well. "Come to think of it, maybe *I'll* sleep."

Zaara waved at them. "Good. Finally, some time alone with my thoughts."

He smiled and made himself comfortable. The world about him began to disintegrate as his eyes closed, and a moment later, he shivered violently. There had been a gust of cold air. How? Where? He tried to open his eyes and couldn't. It wasn't black with them closed. Instead, it was *nothing.*

"Stay calm," Prima said quietly. *"I'm here. You're waking up. You'll be okay, Ben."*

He willed his heart rate to slow and moments later, the nothing disappeared and he opened his eyes to blinding light.

"Ben?" Jacob looked worriedly at him. "How are you feeling?"

"That sucked," he rasped. His throat ached. How long had it been since he had talked? "Waking up, I mean. Well, and some of the story."

"Yeah, sorry." The other man gave him a sympathetic smile as he unhooked monitors. "We knew Zaara was trustworthy, so we never stopped to think that you'd have to consider *her* as a potential assassin. Our bad."

"You seem to have done well, though," said Nick. His face swam into view. He held a hand out. "Here, I'll help you sit."

Ben missed his hand on the first try—his muscles were so sluggish and so exhausted—but he managed on the second and sat with a wince. He tried to scratch his head, which didn't quite work, and stared at his hands.

"What the—"

"Son of a bitch," Jacob said quietly.

He tried to move his hand. "I could do this in the game. Fuck. Fuck!"

"Ah…" The other man couldn't wipe the grin off his face, one shared by Nick. "I don't think you get it, dude." He stepped back at the look Ben gave him. "No, no, listen to me, man. Listen. I get that this is frustrating and you could move around in-game and all that, right? Yeah? But the level of coordination you have right now? You are…easily six to eight months ahead of where we expected you to be."

"What?" He gaped at them.

"Yeah." Jacob continued to grin. He held his hand out for a shake. "And you *earned* it, man. We saw how much you practiced. You put your heart and soul into that, you did the work, and you're doing *incredibly* well."

CHAPTER TWENTY-EIGHT

"Listen, man." Mike's face still showed traces of the sickly yellow-and-purple of a fading bruise. "Anyone can fall. You did. I did. I saw you slip and I could have done ten better things than the one I did. As far as I'm concerned, what matters is that we survived."

Ben nodded.

"And you have *no* idea how good it is to see you moving again," his friend said emphatically.

"Yeah, I..." He shrugged. "It's hard when I was doing so much better in the game and now, I feel like a baby again."

"Miles better than when I saw you," the other man said cheerfully. "Natasha will be pissed that she missed you—I finally got her out of the house instead of hovering over me, and she missed your video call." He paused. "I think maybe I simply won't tell her."

"Honestly? Good plan. She might kill you."

Mike shifted uncomfortably in his chair. His casts were beginning to look dingy. "God, this *itches*. When this started, I only wanted to be able to dance at my wedding. Now, I don't give a damn about that. I simply want the itching to stop. I'd kill a man for that."

"So I should be going," Ben quipped.

The man laughed. "Ohhh, laughing hurts. Anyway. What's the timeline on you coming back out here?"

"Honestly? I'm not sure." He shook his head. "I'm coming along faster than they expected but as you can see, I'm not exactly stable enough to be on my own yet. It also looks like going back into the game will do more for my recovery than anything else."

"What's the game like?" his friend asked him. "You haven't said much about it."

He took a moment to think before he spoke, and he sighed. "I don't know how to describe it. It's more interactive than you'd ever think—it honestly does feel like you're *in* a book or a movie or something. Except it hits harder. *Much* harder. Watching your actions play out, it…humbles you."

Mike guffawed and shook his head.

"What?" He was almost offended.

"That's what this difference has been?" he asked. "You come to me with an apology—and I don't remember the last time you apologized like that, if *ever*—and you're quiet. You're…you, but in a different way. A near-death experience will do that to you, so I didn't think much of it, but from what you're saying, it's the *game* that's changed you."

Ben chewed his lip as he thought this over.

"Like…" Mike had a hard time controlling his amusement. "Fairies and elves and shit? *That* kind of game?"

"You don't understand until you're in it." The words came out of him quickly, and he was surprised by the rush of anger he felt. "They're merely people, Mike, trying to do the best they can— and sometimes, you fuck up and you hurt them and you have to *watch* it."

The man was taken aback and swallowed uncomfortably. "I'm…sorry. I didn't mean—"

"No." He sighed and tried to rub his forehead. When he only succeeded in slinging his arm over one shoulder, it didn't improve his temper. He tried to let the anger dissipate. "I was surprised, too. At the start, I was so aware it was a game and none of it was 'real,' whatever that means, but then I fell into it. So many of my morals were simply...self-centered, and even if it's not real, watching people die violently because you had some idea of moral purity? It...uh, it changes you."

His friend stared at him, wide-eyed. "That sounds...uh, are you sure you want to go back in?"

"Yes," Ben said immediately.

"It doesn't exactly sound pleasant. Like, I'm as happy as anyone that you're feeling better, don't get me wrong, but that sounds really, really...bad." He looked worried.

"I don't think I can explain it," he said after a moment of thought. "You could come see it, I'll bet."

"I'm not sure I want to—and anyway, I can't travel for a while." He looked over his shoulder. "Crap, Natasha's back —gotta go."

He ended the video call with a wave and Ben leaned back in his chair. It was one thing he could do, at least—he simply had to flop backward.

It was difficult to explain what the game had meant to him. His parents hadn't understood either, as much as they approved of the so-called "new Ben" they had seen when they came to visit him. They worried about the violence in the game, not understanding something fundamental about it.

All those things happened in the real world, too.

Sure, there weren't elves or fae, but people did screw one another over and kill for money. Other people—innocent people —were caught in the crossfire. What he hadn't been able to understand when he read about it in the news, he was able to understand when he saw it play out in front of him.

Ben wasn't necessarily looking forward to going back in. The changes he'd seen in himself had been accompanied by a great deal of pain. Shame and self-recrimination were unpleasant, at best. Cutting away the pieces of himself that had given him such certainty was painful. He looked back on things he'd said to friends and he cringed.

When Jacob entered the room, he was still sitting and staring at nothing.

"You'll be pleased to know," the PIVOT CEO told him, "that your test results earned a resounding response from no less than three experts, all accusing us of—I quote—'total bullshit.'" His smile faded at the look on Ben's face. "Are you okay?"

"Um…" He cleared his throat. "Have you had anyone…I don't know how to say this…*change* because of what they saw in the game?"

"Ah." The man put his stack of folders down and pulled a chair closer. "Yes, honestly. We've looked closely at it and it didn't seem way out of line with the effect other art had on people. You've read books before that changed you, right? Seen movies?"

"Never quite as…much," he admitted.

"I get that. You didn't play video games before this, did you?" Jacob waited for his headshake. "I thought not. Putting yourself into the game and being the main character in a different way—it seems to change how people relate to stories."

"That's one way of putting it," he said dryly. He grinned when the other man laughed.

"Oh, and…" Jacob smiled. "Someone is coming to visit you today."

"Really?" His bemusement turned to sudden panic. "Uh, if her name is Eve—"

He had thought about apologizing to her as well but that situation had been both-sided enough that he was content to let sleeping dogs lie. They were better off without one another.

"No." The man looked taken aback. "But we can put an exclusion on your file, you know. Eve?"

"Ex-girlfriend."

"No, I mean what's her surname?" His mouth twitched.

"Oh, right. McClellan." Ben shook his head. "I'm still mushy-brained."

"I can't imagine why." The engineer jotted the name on a post-it. "It's not like you're expending significant energy re-learning how to exist in your body or coping with a near-death experience or anything. It's not like that would…I don't know…take much focus."

"Yeah, yeah." He levered himself up. "So, who's here to see me?"

"You'll see in a minute." Jacob waggled his eyebrows. "I think you'll be happy."

"Fine, fine, keep your secrets." He accepted his help to walk across the room. "You're all dressed up today. Date?"

"No." Surprisingly, the man looked evasive. "Who would I be dating?"

"I thought you were going out with one of the Diatek lawyers."

"What! No. Who told you that?" Jacob gave him a sharp look.

"Um. One of the lab techs, maybe? She seemed very sure."

"Who would have…" He shook his head. "No. I'm not dating anyone."

"Okay." Ben, who had the sense he was wading into somewhat dangerous territory, shut up and hoped his companion would change the subject.

Instead, the man began to walk faster—something he was barely able to keep up with—and flagged Nick down.

"Nick, yo—have you heard any of the lab techs talking about me dating a Diatek lawyer?"

"I've heard talk about it," Nick said. To Ben's eyes, he suddenly looked very uncomfortable.

"*Talk?* Like…like…" Jacob seemed to struggle to find words.

"Who else talked about it?" he asked finally. His voice was far too casual.

Ben, struggling to stay upright, was now definitely sure that he was caught in the middle of something. He hopped to the wall and smiled gratefully when Nick brought him a chair.

"I don't know," Nick said. "Everyone, I guess."

"*Everyone?*"

"Workplace stuff spreads fast."

"But I'm *not* dating anyone!" Jacob waved his hands. "I don't want…anyone…to think that." He looked down the hallway toward the lab.

A suspicion kindled in Ben's head. Did Jacob have the hots for one of the lab techs, maybe? It was possible.

He still wouldn't get involved.

Nick shrugged. "I should get Ben to the lab to see his visitor."

"Huh." Jacob wandered into the break room, muttering to himself.

As they went down the hall, Ben said quietly. "You didn't happen to start that rumor, did you?"

The man did a double-take. "You're good."

"Why?" he asked.

Nick held up one finger for patience and as they entered the main room, gave a tiny nod in Amber's direction. "They needed a nudge," he said under his breath. "Also, it's nice to speak to someone about this before they find out and kill me."

He was still laughing when he saw who had come to visit him.

His jaw dropped.

"And, on a similar note…" Nick said with a meaningful eyebrow waggle. He helped him to a chair. "Can I get you two any coffee or tea?"

Ben's stomach was growling but he couldn't remember the word for food and he didn't even care right now.

"I'll, uh…" Dr. Ullmer looked away from him for long enough to smile at Nick. "I'll take some coffee. Thank you." She was blushing when she looked back. "I hope it's okay that I came to see you."

He tried to come up with words—any words—and couldn't.

Eliza settled herself on one of the chairs and hunched her shoulders. "My sister lives here so I was already coming out. I don't want to seem like a…crazy stalker or anything."

"No! No." He cleared his throat. "Ah…thank you. It is *great* to see you."

Her smile lit her face. "You made quite an impression on all of us and I have to say, I didn't in a million years expect to see you walking already."

"Wait until you watch me try to eat," he said wryly. "Honestly…I'd prefer you didn't watch me try to eat. It's not pretty." *And you are.* No. That was a horrible line. Good Lord.

"Oh. That's kind of a bummer." She bit her lip. "Because the team suggested maybe you'd like to get out of the lab, and I thought…maybe we could…grab a bite." She blushed furiously now.

"Okay, I've…um…" Ben made the mistake of trying to rub his forehead again and this time, hit himself fully in the face. "Ow. Sorry."

"Who are you apologizing to?"

"You. Me. I…I want to be very clear because I've been *super* wrong about this before—ah, are you asking me on a date?"

As soon as the words came out of his mouth, he wanted to hit himself in the face again, deliberately this time. That was the stupidest thing anyone had ever said. Anyone. Ever.

But Eliza smiled and nodded. "Ah, yeah, actually. It would have been wrong for me to do that while you were under my care, but you aren't anymore—and no pressure either." She waved her hands airily.

"I'd love to," Ben said. "Seriously. I'd like that."

A sudden scuffling noise was followed by a yelp, and Nick darted out of the hallway and sprinted desperately to the doorway. He banged out into the hall and fled while they looked blankly after him.

A few seconds later, Jacob and Amber raced after him.

"Ah," He said. "Too bad I can't run. This would be fun to watch."

CHAPTER TWENTY-NINE

"—And now here it is, five years later, and I haven't slept a full night in…a long time." Eliza shrugged and popped a piece of sushi in her mouth. "God, this is good. I gorge myself on sushi every time I'm here. You have no idea. I go home with no savings and no pants that fit." She paused. "I think maybe that's the kind of thing you're not supposed to say on a first date?"

Ben laughed. "I think you're also supposed to be able to eat food on your own, so maybe we're even." He considered the situation with a wry smile. "And, if I'm being frank, finding someone to go out with, gorge ourselves on amazing food, and go home and lie in a heap with and ask each other why we ate so much? That sounds good."

A second later, he realized that he probably shouldn't have mentioned the long term.

"Uh…"

"You're drugged and I'm sleep deprived," she said. "This date will be a shitshow. *However…*" She pointed her chopsticks at him. "I'm having fun."

"I am, too." He needed to change the subject. "Do you think Nick died?"

"Eh?"

"Oh—the guy we saw running."

"Yeah, what was that about?" She snagged another bowl of nigiri off the stream that ran past their table.

"Ah…" Ben explained and took pleasure in the way her face lit up when she laughed.

"Sneaky," she said appreciatively when he'd finished. "I hope he doesn't die. Of course, I've also seen workplace romances turn out badly so I'm not sure how to balance that one. But his heart seems to have been in the right place."

He nodded. From a slow walk around the building—fresh air was good, even when it smelled like exhaust and hot dogs—to this dinner, the afternoon had been amazing. He wanted it to last forever.

It took a few moments to realize that Eliza was staring at him. "Sorry. Did you say something?"

"No, but I noticed you look tired." She smiled encouragingly at him. "Should we get you back?"

"I don't want to go back," he said plaintively.

"You don't?" She raised an eyebrow. "A nice, soft bed. Crisp sheets. A whole night of sleep."

"Stop it," he said, faking drama. "You don't know what you're suggesting."

"Comfy pajamas," Eliza whispered seductively.

"Ugh." He managed to shake a fist. "God forgive me but I'm weak."

"It's not only you. I think I made *myself* a little weak in the knees with that last bit." She grinned. "Shall we?"

"He's *such* a douche," Amber said, for what felt like the fiftieth time. She slumped in her seat and stirred her straw in her milkshake grumpily.

Jacob only nodded grimly and drank his milkshake with a disgruntled expression.

"What was he even *thinking?*" she demanded.

He shrugged, his expression unchanged. Then, he sighed. "Okay, I gotta be honest—I feel like an idiot."

"Oh, me too." She looked at her outfit. "It did get me out of my wardrobe rut and I finally bought new shoes, but *still.*"

"You look good," he said with a half-smile.

"Thanks. You do, too, you know." She laughed, looked at Jacob, and raised a single eyebrow.

He mirrored her.

Neither of them said that this might be a huge mistake or that it would be complicated. They both knew that. Neither of them mentioned that it hadn't worked out the last time. They both knew that, too.

Instead, they both nodded.

"Huh," Amber said.

He put his milkshake down and stood from his chair to lean across the table and kiss her. When she slid her hand around the back of his neck and grinned against his mouth, he smiled.

"Huh?" he echoed when he broke away.

"Uh-huh," Amber said with a nod. "And I suppose we can let the douche live."

"I wouldn't go that far."

"No? He's very useful."

"And a good friend."

"And sneaky. Which can be good."

"Also infuriating, of course."

"Also that."

They frowned in thought before they both nodded again. Nick would get to live.

For now.

Prima watched as Zaara stared into space and cradled a cup of tea in her hands. More and more, the AI tried to watch her characters as the players saw them. It was a fun game to partition the part of herself running the processes that made Zaara and then study the character and wonder what she was thinking.

The woman's despair and determination had worried her when it came to Kural. She was the type of person, Prima thought, who could easily batter herself against the rocks of duty. It was good that she had met Ben and good that he had taken her words to heart, but she was worried that the two of them had only come out of this with different views of morality and not a more forgiving attitude toward their best efforts.

With so little information at their disposal, how could humans ever hold themselves accountable for all the fallout of their actions? And that was even before one counted the cognitive dissonance humans experienced when they faced unpleasant facts.

Prima was rather inclined to think that if she were as limited as a human, she would give up trying to be a good person and live for all the things that provided limbic rewards.

She had been reading up about the human brain.

Whatever the case, she looked forward to having Ben back in the game—as well as a few other visitors.

"Prima?" Taigan called. She had summoned herself a set of stairs that wound around one of the trees. "Can I…see my family?"

It had taken her a long time to work up the courage to ask. She was afraid that the answer would be no, that she wasn't ready yet. Seeing the trees and the sunshine had reminded her of how much she missed and for days, she had scrambled through the forest, swung from vines like Tarzan, and slept on comfy beds that she conjured out of thin air whenever she wanted a nap.

And she had begun to miss her family—not only miss them. She didn't simply want to wake up as an abstract. She had begun to miss them so much that it ached.

"I thought you would never ask," Prima said, amused.

The girl gaped. "You were waiting for me to ask? If I'd asked sooner, I would have gotten to see them sooner? Are you kidding me?"

"In simple terms, your willingness to ask and advocate for yourself, as an expression of your desires, shows a growing awareness and ability to interact."

"Huh?"

"Until you asked, you would not be ready to interact with them."

"I still say it's BS," she muttered.

"That's as may be. Now, I'll need you to head to the mountains on the eastern edge of the forest."

Ben lay on the table. The drugs began to take hold in his blood and he grew sleepier and sleepier.

"So, I'll wake up where I was?"

"Yep." Jacob, who looked a great deal more relaxed this morning—and had broken into a cheerful whistle several times—pushed a few buttons and smiled at him. "Are you ready?"

"There's no time like the present, I suppose." He closed his eyes, breathed in deeply, and opened them to blue.

"You're back!"

"I'm back." Ben sat and his gaze settled on Zaara and Kural sleeping in the litter. "Let's have another adventure."

CREATOR NOTES - MICHAEL ANDERLE

Thank you so much for reading through this story and here to the back for my author notes.

This has been an interesting and educational process for me, trying to reimagine parts of our health care systems.

I understand that so often profit takes the driving seat over benefits to humanity. I am not knocking the reality, I just want to understand it enough to leverage the knowledge.

Perhaps someone reading these stories will have the resources to make this a reality. Point them to where the business can be disrupted, and who knows?

We might get our own version of P.I.V.O.T. Labs.

There are plenty of threads for us to take the stories and continue. However, I have to put out a few fires myself before I get to play again in this world. Who knows, maybe these stories will become sleeper hits and explode humanities consciousness into a whole new realm.

OR (and I find this potentially more likely) someone realizes just how much money IS available to acquire if they fix the ICU area of hospitalization. Let's disrupt the present to build a better future and perhaps I'll get to play in the game myself.

Hopefully as just a consumer, no medical reasons necessary.

Ad Aeternitatem,

Michael Anderle